喚醒你的英文語感!

Get a Feel for English !

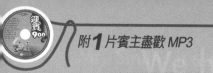

附 **1** 片賓主盡歡 MP3

總編審：王復國
作　者：Brian Greene

迎賓

900 句典。

得罪外賓太離譜

MR SMITH

HLIWS

Mr. Smith

SMITH

☑ 體貼
☑ 溝通
☑ 900句典

貝塔語言出版
Beta Multimedia Publishing

Writer's Introduction

Mr. Smith is coming to town and you have been assigned to be his host. Or perhaps Mrs. Smith is already here and you must show her the sights. Is your English up to the task of making his or her stay memorable and successful without having a heart attack while you are doing it?

No matter what state your English is in, you will find this phrase book helpful and easy to use. It was designed for a Chinese native speaker to comfortably interact with a guest from abroad. Topically organized, there are phrases to use in all kinds of situations with business people, academics, and other visitors from abroad.

Keep in mind that many of the phrases contain nouns and noun phrases that can be substituted with others to suit the context. For example, on topic 106, you will find the phrase "We'll have dinner with the technology people at 6:30 or 7:00." Most likely, this meal has been arranged to help your guest satisfy a particular objective. If your guest is an academic trying to get permission to enter an archive, you could fine-tune the noun phrase at the end of the sentence and say, "We'll have lunch with the archive director at 12:30." On the other hand, if your guest is doing business, then perhaps it would be more appropriate to say, "We'll have dinner with a couple of guys from the marketing department at around 7:30."

Another feature of this book is the names of people, companies, and places that are used. We kept them simple and few to make it easier for you to replace them with the relevant names particular to your circumstances, and to more clearly see the functional patterns in the phrases. This, we hope, will increase the effectiveness of the book as a tool for communication and language learning.

In addition, strategies for using English have been included. Since a single book cannot possibly contain all of the things a foreign guest might happen to say to a host, you need to know how to tactfully handle instances of not understanding to avoid misunderstanding. For example, on topic 98 you will find the phrase, "Lip balm? What does it look like?" This teaches the skill of repeating a noun or noun phrase and following it with a question to cope with something you do not understand.

Hosting a guest from abroad requires preparation and hard work. With its emails and phrases to use for planning, executing, and concluding a guest's stay, *Overheard While Entertaining Guests* should be within reach when the time comes to host Mr. or Mrs. Smith — no matter from where he or she arrives, or to where you decide to take him or her. Good luck.

作者序

　　史密斯先生就要到了,而你被指派作接待人。或者史密斯太太人已經到了,而你必須帶她到各處參觀。你的英語能力是否足以讓對方此行圓滿成功並留下難忘的回憶,同時你又不會緊張到心臟病發作?

　　無論你目前的英語程度如何,你會發現這本句典既實用,使用上又方便。本書針對以中文為母語的人士而設計,教你如何從容應對國外訪客。本書的內容安排採主題式設計,適用於接待國外商務人士、學術界人士或其他領域訪客的各種場合。

　　提醒讀者:你可以依據場合,將本書許多句子中的名詞和名詞片語,用其他的名詞和名詞片語來代替。例如,主題 106 中有一句是 "We'll have dinner with the technology people at 6:30 or 7:00."「我們六點半或七點和技術部門的人晚餐有約。」安排這頓飯局的用意極有可能是為了協助你的訪客達成某個目的。假設你的訪客是學術界人士,想取得某一資料庫的使用權,此時你可以在句末的名詞片語上作細微調整,你可以說:"We'll have lunch with the archive director at 12:30."「我們十二點半和資料庫的主任午餐有約。」換個角度,假使你的訪客是商場人士,此時這樣說或許更為恰當:"We'll have dinner with a couple of guys from the marketing department at around 7:30."「我們七點半和幾位行銷部門的人晚餐有約。」

　　本書中使用的人名、公司名、地名是本書的另一項特色。我們盡量採用簡單的名字,數量也不算多,讀者可以考量個人的情形替之以相關的名稱;此外,讀者還可以清楚地看出這些句子的結構是具功能性的。

我們希望這樣的設計能讓本書成為讀者在溝通和語言學習上最有效率的利器。

此外，本書還教你使用英語時的一些訣竅。因為單單一本書不可能收錄國外訪客可能對招待人說的所有話語，因此你必須知道在不瞭解對方意思時，該如何巧妙應對以避免誤會。例如：主題 98 中你會看到這個句子：Lip balm? What does it look like?"「護唇膏？長什麼樣子？」這種句法教你在遇到不知道的事情時，先複述該名詞或名詞片語，然後再問問題的技巧。

迎接國外賓客需要事先準備並下苦工。《迎賓 900 句典》設計的電子郵件範例和用語，適用於外賓造訪時行程上的安排、接待、和送別。無論是要招待史密斯先生還是史密斯太太、無論對方打從哪裡來、無論你決定帶對方上哪去，這本書都很容易上手。祝學習順利！

CONTENTS

Part 3 抵達與就緒

Part 4 食物和飲料

Part 6 觀光、活動、娛樂

Part 7 購物

Part 8 任務開始

Part 9 解決問題

Part **1**

事先安排
Pre-visit Arrangements

1 邀請：簡短通報
Making an Invitation : Simple Announcements

☐ You are cordially[1] invited to attend the fifth annual[2] NMA conference.[3]

誠摯地邀請您參加第五屆 NMA 年度會議。

☐ The department of history invites you to attend this year's research workshop.

歷史系邀請您參加本年度的研討會。

☐ We really hope you will be able to attend.

我們很希望您能夠參加。

☐ We are pleased to announce[4] your application has been accepted.

我們很高興通知您，您的申請已經通過了。

☐ On behalf of all of us in the planning department, I look forward to your visit.

我代表企劃部全體人員，期待您的出席。

☐ Everyone here at Yoyodyne is enthusiastic[5] to meet your team.

友友戴恩的每位成員都非常期待和您的團隊會面。

Word List

1 cordially [`kɔrdʒəlɪ] adv. 誠摯地
2 annual [`ænjuəl] adj. 一年一次的
3 conference [`kɑnfərəns] n. 會議
4 announce [ə`naʊns] v. 通報
5 enthusiastic [ɪn.θjuzɪ`æstɪk] adj. 熱烈的

2 邀請：說明時間和地點

🎧 **MP3** 03

Making an Invitation : Specifying the Time and Place

時間 ☐ The workshop will run from Monday, July 5 to Sunday, July 11, 2010.

研討會時間將從 2010 年 7 月 5 日星期一進行到 7 月 11 日星期日。

☐ The committee[1] welcomes you to join our training session[2] this spring.

委員會歡迎您加入我們今年春季的培訓班。

地點 ☐ This year's event will be held at the Chunghua Convention[3] Center.

本年度的活動將在中華會議中心舉辦。

☐ The site of the seminar is conveniently located in central Taipei.

研討會的地點位於交通便利的台北市中心。

時間和 ☐ The conference will be held next year in Taipei from May 1 to 5.
地點
會議將於明年 5 月 1 日到 5 日在台北舉辦。

☐ Our R&D team will demo[4] the product to invited guests at our Hsinchu headquarters[5] on July 18. It would be great if you could make it.

我們的研發部 7 月 18 日將在新竹總公司為受邀來賓進行產品示範說明。如果您能夠出席將會是我們的榮幸。

Word List

1 committee [kəˋmɪtɪ] n. 委員會
2 session [ˋsɛʃən] n. 講習會
3 convention [kənˋvɛnʃən] n. 會議
4 demo [ˋdɛmo] v. (=demonstrate [ˋdɛmənˌstret]) 產品示範操作
5 headquarters [ˋhɛdˋkwɔrtəz] n. 總公司

3 確認訊息
Confirming Information

🎧 MP3 04

☐ Please confirm your arrival[1] and departure[2] times as soon as possible.

請儘快確認您的抵達和離去時間。

☐ You will be arriving on Wednesday, October 14 at 6:30 p.m., correct?

您將會在 10 月 14 日星期三晚上六點半抵達，正確嗎？

☐ I just want to make sure that there are fourteen people in your group, including you.

我只想確定一下您團上包括您在內，一共是十四個人。

☐ You mentioned you might be arriving a few days late. Is that still the case?

您提過可能會晚幾天到。現在是否還是如此？

☐ Just checking to see if you and Steve Smith will still be arriving separately.[3]

只想跟您確認一下，您和史帝夫・史密斯是否仍然會分別到達。

☐ Daphne Yang emailed saying your presentation may change. Please confirm this.

黛芬妮・楊寄電子郵件告知說您的簡報內容可能會更動。請確認這一點。

Word List

[1] arrival [əˋraɪvl] n. 到達
[2] departure [dɪˋpartʃə] n. 出發；啟程
[3] separately [ˋsɛpərɪtlɪ] adv. 分別地

4 提出請求
Making Requests

 MP3 05

☐ Please fax us a copy of your passport. The number is 886-02-2312-3535.

請把您的護照傳真一份給我們。電話號碼是 886-02-2312-3535.。

☐ Can you send me a copy of your itinerary?[1]

可不可以把您的行程表寄給我一份？

☐ Please confirm how many will be in your party.

請確認您一行人的人數。

☐ Would it be possible to fax another copy of your visa? The first one was unclear.[2]

可不可能再傳真一次您的簽證？第一次傳的不清楚。

☐ Could you give me your fax number?

您可不可以將傳真號碼給我？

☐ Please forward[3] your CV[4] or resume[5] to us as soon as possible.

請儘快將您的簡歷或履歷表寄給我們。

Word List

1 itinerary [aɪˋtɪnəˌrɛrɪ] n. 行程表
2 unclear [ʌnˋklɪr] adj. 不清楚的
3 forward [ˋfɔrwəd] v. 轉寄

4 CV n. (=curriculum vitae [kəˋrɪkjələmˋvaɪti]) 簡歷表
5 resume [ˌrɛzjuˋme] n. 履歷表

5 運籌：行程安排

Logistics[1]: Scheduling

☐ Blake Chen will greet you at the airport when you arrive March 10.

您 3 月 10 日抵達時，布萊克‧陳會到機場迎接。

☐ I've arranged a mini van to take you from the airport to the hotel.

我已經安排了一部小巴士，會從機場把您載送到飯店。

☐ There's been a slight[2] change. You'll stay at the Hyatt the first night, then move to the Westin.

我們做了一些更動。您頭一晚將下榻君悅飯店，之後再轉往六福皇宮飯店。

☐ Would it be OK if I met you at your hotel Thursday morning at 9:30?

星期四早上九點半我跟您在您的飯店碰面好不好？

☐ We'd like you to give a short speech on the morning of the 6th.

我們希望您在第六天上午做個簡短的演講。

☐ We hope you can give a brief overview[3] presentation on Monday after you arrive.

我們希望在您抵達之後，可以在星期一做個簡短的摘要報告。

Word List

1 logistics [loˋdʒɪstɪks] n. 運籌
2 slight [slaɪt] adj. 輕微的
3 overview [ˋovəˌvju] n. 概要；綜述

6 運籌：付款和行政作業

🎧 MP3 07

Logistics : Payments and Paperwork

☐ Please send a (non-refundable[1]) deposit[2] of US$100 by August 20.
請在 8 月 20 日之前匯入美金一百元的訂金（不退還）。

☐ Please submit[3] payment by international money order, made payable[4] to Yoyodyne.
請用國際匯票付款，受款人載明為友友戴恩公司。

☐ Kindly return the attached form no later than January 15.
請於 1 月 15 日之前將附上的表格寄回來。

☐ The deadline for submitting the information is Friday, April 8.
繳交資料的期限是 4 月 8 日星期五。

☐ Cab fare from the airport to our office will be about NT$1,000. Give the driver the address below.
從機場到我們公司的計程車資大約是新台幣一千元。將下列地址交給司機。

☐ Please click on the link below to see a printable map of the campus and surrounding[5] area.
請點擊下方連結地址，您會看到有校區和附近一帶的地圖可供列印。

Word List

1 non-refundable [ˌnɑnrɪˋfʌndəbl]
adj. 不可退費的

2 deposit [dɪˋpɑzɪt] n. 訂金；押金

3 submit [səbˋmɪt] v. 繳交；送出

4 payable [ˋpeəbl] adj. 可支付的

5 surrounding [səˋraundɪŋ] adj. 周遭的

Part 2

電子郵件樣本
Sample Email

7 電子郵件樣本：邀請
Sample Email : Invitation

MP3 08

From : Christine Chow
To : Professor Smith

Dear Professor Smith,

The Ministry of Transportation[1] cordially invites you to attend the MoT research conference from April 15 through April 20. At your earliest convenience, please fill out the attached form and return it via fax or email. Hotel reservations[2] will be made on your behalf.[3]

As soon as you have booked your flight, please forward your itinerary so that arrangements can be made to meet you at the airport.

We look forward to your visit.

Cordially,

Christine Chow
Committee Chairman

7 電子郵件樣本：邀請
Sample Email : Invitation

寄件人：克莉斯汀・周
收件人：史密斯教授

史密斯教授您好：

交通部誠摯地邀請您參加於 4 月 15 日到 20 日所舉辦的交通部研討會。如果您方便的話，請儘早將附上的表格填妥，然後以傳真或電子郵件回覆。我們會代您訂飯店房間。

您的機位一訂好，就請將您的行程傳給我們，以便我們安排接機事宜。

期待您的到訪。

委員會主席

克莉斯汀・周
謹上

List

1 transportation [ˌtrænspɚˋteʃən]
n. 交通；運輸

2 reservation [ˌrɛzɚˋveʃən]
n. 房間或席位的預定

3 on one's behalf [bɪˋhæf] 代表某人做某事

電子郵件樣本：確認
Sample Email : Confirmation

From : Shannon Wu
To : Mr. Smith

Dear Mr. Smith,

On behalf of all of us at Yoyodyne, we look forward to your visit.

Please confirm that you will arrive Wednesday, November 1 at 6:20 p.m. on Cathay Pacific flight CX460.

Edward Yang from the sales department will meet you at the airport and take you to your hotel after your arrival.

There has been a slight change to the agenda[1] of the meeting for the morning of November 3. Please see the attachment for details.

If you have any questions, don't hesitate[2] to contact me.

Sincerely,

Shannon Wu
Senior Engineer[3]

8 電子郵件樣本：確認
Sample Email : Confirmation

寄件人：夏農·吳
收件人：史密斯

史密斯先生您好：

我們謹代表友友戴恩全體員工期待您的到訪。
請確認您將搭乘國泰航空 **CX 460** 班機於 **11** 月 **1** 日星期三晚上 **6** 點 **20** 分抵達。

業務部的愛德華·楊會到機場接機並在您抵達後帶您到飯店。 **11** 月 **3** 日早上的會議議程有些微更動，詳情請參閱附檔。
如果您有任何疑問，儘管和我聯絡。

資深工程師

夏農·吳
敬上·

Word
List

1 agenda [ə`dʒɛndə] n. 會議的議程
2 hesitate [`hɛzə‚tet] v. 猶豫
3 engineer [‚ɛndʒə`nɪr] n. 工程師

9 電子郵件樣本：請求

Sample Email : Request

From : Ben Wang, ph.D.
To : Professor Cook

Dear Professor Cook,

We are thrilled[1] to be able to host[2] your students this summer from July 4 to September 2.

If you would, please make sure each student brings two (2), two-inch (2") passport-sized photos. They will be used for library cards and student IDs. As per[3] our email of June 8, each student will be responsible[4] for a room deposit of NT$1,500, and a key deposit of NT$500.

A campus representative[5] will greet you at the airport and bring you to the campus on a private bus.

When the student roster[6] is finalized, please send it to Daphne Yang (dyang@ntu.edu.tw).

Regards,

Ben Wang, ph.D.
International Student Affairs

9 電子郵件樣本：請求
Sample Email : Request

寄件人：班・王博士
收件人：庫克教授

庫克教授您好：

我們非常高興能在今年夏天 7 月 4 日到 9 月 2 日招待您的學生。

麻煩您，請務必通知每位同學攜帶兩張兩吋護照規格的照片，以便製作圖書證和學生證。我們在 6 月 8 日的電子郵件中有提到，每位同學要繳交房間訂金台幣一千五百元、鑰匙訂金台幣五百元。

屆時會有一位校園代表在機場迎接你們，並帶大家搭乘民營巴士到學校。

在學生名冊確定之後，請寄給黛芬妮・楊小姐（**dyang@ntu.edu.tw**）。

國際學生事務處

班・王博士
謹啟

Word List

1 thrilled [θrɪld] adj. 非常高興的
2 host [host] v. 主辦；主持；招待
3 As per prep.（非正式）根據；按照
4 responsible [rɪ`spɑnsəbl] adj. 負責
5 representative [rɛprɪ`zɛntətɪv] n. 代表
6 roster [`rɑstə] n. 名冊

From : Brad
To : Paul

Dear Paul,

Two quick questions for you:

1. I'm wondering if you plan on bringing the prototype[1] with you to the trade show?[2]

2. Will you be able to bring that other software that we discussed over the phone last Tuesday (March 20)?

Let me know as soon as it's convenient.

Thanks,

Brad

10 電子郵件樣本：詢問
Sample Email : Inquiry

寄件人：布萊德
收件人：保羅

保羅您好：

兩個簡單的問題想請教您：

一、我在想不知道您是否會把原型帶到商品展場來？

二、您是否可以把我們上星期二（3 月 20 日）在電話中討論到的另一個
　　軟體帶過來？

如果方便，請儘早通知我。

多謝。

布萊德

1 prototype [ˋprotəˌtaɪp] n. 原型
2 trade show 商品展

Part3

抵達與就緒
Arrival and Settling In

11 在機場尋找來賓 I

Finding Your Guest(s) at the Airport I

以下情形適用於你無法確認是否等對了人。

☐ Excuse me, are you Ms. Smith?

對不起,請問你是史密斯女士嗎?

☐ Hi there. Would you be Ms. Smith from Yoyodyne Ltd.?

你好,請問您是不是友友戴恩公司的史密斯女士?

☐ Pardon me. You don't happen to be[1] Cynthia Smith, by any chance?[2]

對不起。您該不會碰巧就是辛西亞・史密斯吧?

☐ Hello. I'm looking for Ms. Cynthia Smith from Everglade College.

哈囉!我在找埃佛格萊德大學的辛西亞・史密斯女士。

☐ I'm here to meet a group from Everglade College. Are you with them?

我來這裡迎接來自埃佛格萊德大學的一行人。你和他們是不是一道的?

☐ I'm sorry. Are you part of the theater group from Holland?

對不起,請問您是不是來自荷蘭的戲劇表演團體成員之一?

Word List

1 happen to be 碰巧是……
2 by any chance 碰巧

12 在機場尋找來賓 II

 MP3 13

Finding Your Guest(s) at the Airport II

以下情形適用於你確定等對了人。

☐ Hello! Mr. Smith!

哈囉！史密斯先生！

☐ Mr. Smith. Over here!

史密斯先生。我在這邊！

☐ Mr. Smith. This way please.

史密斯先生，請走這邊。

☐ You must be Mr. Smith.

你一定就是史密斯先生。

☐ Mr. Smith. I'm Edward Yang. We spoke on the phone.

史密斯先生，我是愛德華‧楊。我們通過電話。

☐ Mr. Smith. It's nice to finally meet you in person.[1] I'm Edward Yang.

史密斯先生，真高興終於見到您本人。我是愛德華‧楊。

Word List

1 in person 親自；與人面對面

13 問候 I
Greetings I

☐ Welcome to Taiwan.

歡迎到台灣來。

☐ Hello, Mr. Smith. Welcome to Taipei. I'm Kate Yang.

哈囉，史密斯先生，歡迎到台北來。我是凱蒂‧楊。

☐ Here's my card.

這是我的名片。

☐ Let me help you with your bag.

我來幫你提袋子。

☐ We have a car waiting outside.

我們有部車在外面等候。

☐ Please come with me.

請跟我來。

14 問候 II
Greetings II

MP3 15

等候   ☐ Sorry for keeping you waiting.[1]

抱歉讓您等候多時。

☐ I'm sorry. I was waiting at the wrong exit.[2]

對不起，我剛跑錯出口等候。

☐ I hope you haven't been waiting long.

希望我沒讓你等很久。

班機   ☐ How long was your flight?

這趟飛機坐了多久？

☐ I hope you had a comfortable[3] flight.

希望這趟飛行旅途舒適。

☐ I'm sorry to hear you had such a bad flight.

聽到您這趟飛行旅途不太順利，我覺得很遺憾。

Word List

1 keep sb. waiting 讓某人久等
2 exit [`ɛgzɪt] *n.* 出口
3 comfortable [`kʌmfətəbl] *adj.* 舒適的

Part 3 抵達與就緒

15 介紹其他人 I

Introducing Others I

以下適用於雙方初次見面，以及再次見面的介紹。

☐ Ms. Smith, I'd like you to meet Paul Liu. Paul, this is Cynthia Smith.

史密斯女士，這位是保羅・劉先生。保羅，這位是辛西亞・史密斯。

☐ Ms. Smith is visiting us from London. She's with Yoyodyne.

史密斯女士是從倫敦來的。她在友友戴恩公司服務。

☐ Paul will be your point of contact during your stay.

保羅將是您停留這段時間的聯絡人。

☐ Cynthia, it's so nice to see you again.

辛西亞，很高興再見到您。

☐ Paul, I believe you already know Cynthia.

保羅，我相信你已經認識辛西亞。

☐ Cynthia, you remember Paul from the last trade show?

辛西亞，您還記得上次在商品展場上見過的保羅嗎？

16 介紹其他人 II
Introducing Others II

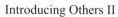

包括職銜、領域、專業能力。

☐ Doctor Smith is a professor of economics at Everglade University in Florida.

史密斯博士是佛州埃佛葛萊德大學的經濟學教授。

☐ Please just call me Colin.

請叫我柯林就行了。

☐ Ms. Smith is the managing director[1] of the dance troupe.[2]

史密斯女士是舞蹈團的總監。

☐ Mr. Smith, this is my manager, Ms. Wang.

史密斯先生,這是我的經理王女士。

☐ Professor Wang is the head of the department and director of the program.

王教授是我們這個系的主任,也是這項計畫的負責人。

☐ Ms. Wang is our chief engineer on the project.

王女士是我們這項企畫的執行工程師。

Word List

[1] managing director [ˈmænɪdʒɪŋ dəˈrɛktə] *n.* 總監
[2] dance troupe [trup] *n.* 舞蹈團

行李
問題

☐ Let me talk to the airline about your luggage.[1]
我去跟航空公司問問你的行李。

☐ Your bag will be delivered[2] to your hotel later tonight.
你的行李袋今天晚上稍晚會送到你下榻的飯店。

生病

☐ We could stop by a pharmacy[3] on the way to the hotel.
去飯店途中我們可以順便到一家藥局。

☐ Let me take you to see a doctor.
我帶你去看醫生。

兌換
錢幣

☐ Would you like to exchange[4] some money?
你想要兌換一些錢嗎？

☐ The exchange rate at the airport is about the same as at the hotel.
機場的兌換匯率和飯店的大致相同。

Word List

1 luggage [ˋlʌgɪdʒ] *n.* 行李
2 deliver [dɪˋlɪvɚ] *v.* 遞送

3 pharmacy [ˋfɑrməsɪ] *n.* 藥局
4 exchange [ɪksˋtʃendʒ] *v.* 交換；兌換

18 解決問題 II
Problem Solving II

🎧 **MP3** 19

有人走失 □ Someone in your group is missing? I'll have him/her paged.[1]

您團上有人走失了？我來用廣播找他／她。

□ Someone in your party is still in immigration?[2] What's his/her name?

你們這一團還有人在入境管理處嗎？他／她叫什麼名字？

遺失物品 □ One of your students has lost a laptop?[3] What kind was it?

您的學生中有人遺失了筆記型電腦？是哪一種的？

□ Did you leave it on the plane or lose it in the terminal?[4]

您的東西是遺忘在飛機上，還是掉在航站裡？

聯絡 □ Would you like to rent a cell phone to use while you're in Taipei?

您在台北這段期間要不要租一支手機？

□ If you'd like to make a call, you're welcome to use my phone.

如果您需要打電話，可以使用我的手機。

Word List

1 page [pedʒ] *v.* 廣播呼叫（找）某人
2 immigration [ˌɪməˈgreʃən]
　　n. 入境管理（檢查）
3 laptop [ˈlæpˌtɑp] *n.* 膝上型電腦
4 terminal [ˈtɜmən!] *n.* 機場航站

Part 3 抵達與就緒

19 確保訪客賓至如歸
Making Sure Your Guest Is Comfortable

☐ **Is there anything I can get for you?**
我可以幫你拿點什麼嗎？

☐ **I brought some water. Would you like some?**
我拿了些茶水來。您想不想喝點水？

☐ **Would you care for¹ something to drink?**
您要不要喝點什麼？

☐ **Would you like to sit down and rest² for a few minutes?**
您要不要坐下來休息幾分鐘？

☐ **Do you have a coat? It's pretty cold outside.**
您有外套嗎？外面非常冷。

☐ **Paul will take care of³ your luggage.**
保羅會處理您的行李。

Word List

1 Would you care for... 你想不想要……
2 rest [rɛst] *v.* 休息
3 take care of 照顧；負責；處理

20 機場的交通工具

Transportation from the Airport

公車 ☐ The bus will take us right[1] to the hotel.

這輛巴士會直接載我們去飯店。

☐ Wait here for just a minute. I'm going to buy our bus tickets.

在這裡等一下。我要去買我們的巴士車票。

計程車 ☐ We'll be taking a taxi, Ms. Smith.

史密斯女士,我們會搭計程車。

☐ We'll put your luggage in the trunk.[2]

我們會把您的行李放在行李箱內。

汽車 ☐ There's a car waiting at the curb,[3] Mr. Smith.

史密斯先生,有輛車在路緣等候。

☐ My car is in the parking lot.[4]

我的車在停車場。

Word List

[1] right [raɪt] *adv.* 直接地
[2] trunk [trʌŋk] *n.* 汽車車後的行李箱
[3] curb [kɜb] *n.* 路緣;人行道旁的砌石邊
[4] parking lot *n.* 停車場

21 閒聊：交通

Small Talk : Transportation[1]

☐ It'll take us about thirty minutes to get to the hotel.

我們到飯店大約要半小時。

☐ The airport is about forty kilometers from downtown.

機場到市中心大約是四十公里。

☐ We'll probably hit[2] some traffic once[3] we get into the city.

我們一旦進入市區就可能會碰到塞車。

☐ At this time of day there shouldn't be any traffic.

一天的這個時候應該不會塞車。

☐ Actually, the traffic situation is much better now than it was a few years ago.

其實，現在的交通狀況和幾年前比起來好很多了。

☐ Be careful crossing[4] the streets. We've got some crazy drivers here.

過馬路的時候請小心。我們這裡有一些瘋狂的駕駛人。

Word List

1 transportation [ˌtrænspɚˋteʃən] *n.* 交通運輸
2 hit [hɪt] *v.* 【口語】遇到；碰到
3 once [wʌns] *conj.* 一旦
4 cross [krɔs] *v.* 穿越

22 閒聊：天氣和一般計畫

Small Talk : Weather and General Plans

MP3 23

天氣 ☐ You've come at the right/wrong time of the year.
你來對／錯季節了。

☐ It's probably going to be cloudy all week.
這整個禮拜可能都會是陰天。

☐ It might take a while to get used to[1] the humidity.[2]
可能要花一些時間才能習慣潮濕的氣候。

一般
計畫
☐ Is this your first time here?
這是您第一次到此地嗎？

☐ If there's anything special you'd like to do while you're here, just let me know.
在此地的期間，您如果想要做什麼特別的事，儘管告訴我。

☐ If you have any free time, I'd be happy to show you around.[3]
如果您有空，我很樂意帶您到處逛逛。

Word List

[1] get used to 習慣於
[2] humidity [hjuˋmɪdətɪ] *n.* 潮濕；濕氣
[3] show sb. around 帶某人到處逛逛

23 在飯店：抵達和投宿
At the Hotel : Arriving and Checking In

☐ Here we are.

我們到了。

☐ I'll take care of your luggage.

我會處理您的行李。

☐ Let me help you check in.

我來幫您辦理入宿。

☐ You're going to need to fill out[1] this form.

您必須填妥這張表格。

☐ They need your passport and a credit card.

他們需要您的護照和信用卡。

☐ Please sign[2] your name here.

請在這裡簽上您的名字。

Word List

[1] fill out 填寫
[2] sign [saɪn] v. 簽名

24 在飯店：設備和運籌

At the Hotel : Facilities[1] and Logistics[2]

設備   ☐ There is a complimentary[3] breakfast from 7:00 until 10:30.

七點到十點半有免費的早餐。

☐ Your room has (wireless) Internet access.

您的房間可以（無線）上網。

☐ The laundry room is in the basement.

洗衣間在地下室。

運籌   ☐ If you need anything, just call me.

如果您需要任何東西，儘管打電話給我。

☐ This card has the hotel address. Use it if you're lost or take a taxi.

這張卡片上有飯店的地址。若您迷路了或者搭計程車時可使用。

☐ We've got a big day tomorrow. You'd better get some rest.

我們明天會非常忙碌。您最好先休息一下。

Word List

[1] facilities [fə`sɪlətɪz]
    n. 【複數形】設備；設施
[2] logistics [lo`dʒɪstɪks] *n.* 運籌

[3] complimentary [ˌkɑmplə`mɛntərɪ]
    adj. 免費贈送的

Part *3* 抵達與就緒

25 聊聊自己
Talking About Yourself

在你的訪客抵達後，雙方更進一步認識。訪客可能會問你一些問題，例如「跟我說說關於你自己的事。」

☐ I was born and raised[1] in Kaohsiung.
我是在高雄出生長大的。

☐ I majored[2] in English in college and spent a year in Canada.
我大學時主修英文，並在加拿大待過一年。

☐ I've been working at Yoyodyne for two and a half years.
我已經在友友戴恩工作了兩年半。

☐ Before I joined Yoyodyne, I worked with TwinStar for about three years.
我到友友戴恩上班之前，在雙子星工作了大約三年。

☐ I like reading, traveling, and gardening.[3]
我喜歡閱讀、旅行、還有園藝。

Word List

1 raise [rez] *v.* 養育
2 major [`medʒɚ] *v.* 主修
3 gardening [`gɑrdn̩ɪŋ] *n.* 園藝

26 聊聊你的家人
Talking About Your Family

☐ I just got engaged[1] last year. I plan to get married next spring.

我去年才訂婚。我打算明年春天結婚。

☐ I don't have any kids yet, but I'm planning on it.

我還沒有小孩,但我正在計畫中。

☐ My sister has four kids. My nieces[2] and nephews[3] are cute, but they are a lot of work.

我的姊姊有四個小孩。我的姪女和姪子們很可愛,但是他們挺麻煩的。

☐ I have two boys. Eight and eleven. They're a real handful.[4]

我有兩個男孩,八歲和十一歲。他們實在很不聽話。

☐ I have a twenty-year-old daughter. She's studying in France.

我有個二十歲的女兒,她在法國唸書。

☐ My son and daughter are three years apart.[5]

我的兒子和女兒相差三歲。

Word List

1 engage [ɪnˋgedʒ] *v.* 訂婚
2 niece [nis] *n.* 姪女;外甥女
3 nephew [ˋnɛfju] *n.* 姪兒;外甥
4 handful [ˋhændfʊl] *adj.* 【口語】難控制的人;棘手的事
5 apart [əˋpart] *adv.* 相隔

Part 4

食物和飲料
Food and Drink

27 詢問你的訪客會不會餓或口渴 MP3 28

Asking If Your Guest Is Hungry or Thirsty

食物 ☐ Are you feeling hungry yet?

您覺得餓了嗎？

☐ How hungry are you?

您有多餓？（您會不會很餓？）

☐ You must be starving.[1]

您一定餓壞了。

飲料 ☐ Can I get you a cup of coffee or tea?

要不要我幫您拿杯咖啡或茶？

☐ Would you like something to drink?

您想不想喝點什麼？

☐ I'm getting a little thirsty. How about you?

我覺得有點渴。您呢？

Word
List

1 starve [stɑrv] v.（使）挨餓

28 邀請你的訪客用餐
Inviting Your Guest to a Meal

MP3 29

☐ Do you feel like getting something to eat?

您想不想吃點東西？

☐ How about some breakfast (lunch/dinner)?

我們用點早餐（中餐／晚餐），如何？

☐ Do you have time for a quick bite?[1]

您有時間簡單吃一下嗎？

☐ Are you ready for lunch?

您準備好吃午餐了嗎？

☐ What would you like to eat?

您想吃點什麼？

☐ There's a really good noodle restaurant near here. Would you like to go?

這附近有家麵店非常好吃。您想不想去？

---

[1] bite [baɪt] n. 【口語】食物

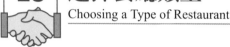
☐ What kind of place would you like to go? Sit-down or something fast?

您想去什麼樣的地方？是可以坐下來用餐的，還是速戰速決的？

☐ There are several restaurants here in the hotel.

這飯店裡有幾間餐廳。

☐ How about a Chinese buffet[1] place?

去中式自助餐館吃如何？

☐ Maybe we should grab[2] a snack[3] at a night market?

或許我們應該去夜市隨意吃個小吃？

☐ If you're hungry, I know a good all-you-can-eat[4] restaurant.

如果您餓了，我知道有一家吃到飽的餐廳很好吃。

☐ Are you up for[5] something totally local? I've got a place in mind that's good and cheap.

您要不要嘗試道地的小吃呢？我知道有一家好吃又便宜。

Word List

[1] buffet [bʊˋfe] n. 自助餐
[2] grab [græb] v. 抓取；匆忙地做
[3] snack [snæk] n. 點心；小吃

[4] all-you-can-eat 吃到飽
[5] Are you up for...? 你有沒有興趣……？

30 選擇各國或地方性的佳餚

Choosing a National or Regional Cuisine[1]

☐ How does Japanese food sound?

去吃日本料理如何？

☐ There is a good Italian place not far from here.

有家好吃的義大利餐館離這裡不遠。

☐ How about Korean barbeque?

吃韓國烤肉如何？

☐ I'd like to take you to Mongolian[2] hot pot.[3] I think you'll like it.

我想帶您去吃蒙古火鍋。我想您會喜歡的。

☐ Let's have a traditional Chinese breakfast.

我們去吃傳統的中式早餐吧。

☐ If you'd like Western food, I know just the place.

如果您想吃西式料理，我知道咱們該上哪去。

Part 4 食物和飲料

Word List

1 cuisine [kwɪˋzin] n. 菜餚；烹飪
2 Mongolian [mɑŋˋgoljən] adj. 蒙古（人）的
3 hot pot 火鍋

31 詢問食物偏好

Asking About Food Preferences[1]

☐ What kind of food do you like?

您喜歡哪種料理？

☐ Is Chinese food OK? Or would you rather have something else?

中式料理可以嗎？還是您想吃點別的？

☐ Is there anything you'd especially like to try?

您有沒有特別想嘗試的東西？

☐ How about seafood?

吃海鮮如何？

☐ Do you like spicy[2] food?

您喜歡辣的食物嗎？

☐ Would you mind having something deep-fried?[3]

您介不介意吃油炸的食物？

Word List

❶ preference [`prɛfərəns] n. 偏愛的事物或人
❷ spicy [`spaɪsɪ] adj. 辛辣的
❸ deep-fried [`dip`fraɪd] adj. 油炸的

☐ Is there anything you'd rather not eat?

有沒有什麼是您不吃的？

☐ Are you a vegetarian/[2]vegan?[3]

您吃素嗎？

☐ Do you have any dietary[4] restrictions?

您是否有任何飲食禁忌？

☐ Are you allergic[5] to anything?

您有沒有對什麼東西過敏？

☐ Are you up for trying something a little unusual?

您有沒有興趣嘗試一點特別的？

☐ Should I ask them not to use MSG?[6]

需要我吩咐他們不要加味精嗎？

Part 4 食物和飲料

Word List

1 restriction [rɪˋstrɪkʃən] n. 限制；約束
2 vegetarian [ˏvɛdʒəˋtɛrɪən] n. 素食者
3 vegan [ˋvɛgən]
　　n. 嚴守素食主義的人；純素食者

4 dietary [ˋdaɪəˏtɛrɪ] adj. 飲食的
5 allergic [əˋlɜdʒɪk] adj. 過敏的
6 MSG 味精（為 monosodium glutamate
　　[ˏmɑnəˋsodɪəm ˋglutəˏmet] 的簡稱）

小吃
- braised[1] pork rice 滷肉飯
- duck with ginger[2] 薑母鴨
- egg cake (danbing) 蛋餅
- oyster[3] omelet[4]/vermicelli[5]
  蚵仔煎 / 麵線
- pig's blood cake 豬血糕
- salty rice pudding 碗粿

- spring roll(s) 春捲
- steamed[6] sandwich 割包
- stewed[7] lamb 羊肉爐
- stinky[8] tofu 臭豆腐
- Taiwanese meatball(s) 肉圓
- thick pork soup/noodles
  肉羹湯／麵

傳統菜
- boiled[9] dumpling(s)
  (shuijiao) 水餃
- glutinous[10] oil rice 油飯

- noodles with marinated[11]
  meat sauce 炸醬麵
- rice dumpling(s) (zongzi) 肉粽

甜點和飲料
- pearl[12] milk tea 珍珠奶茶
- tofu pudding 豆花

- vegetarian gelatin[13] 愛玉
- tomatoes on sticks 糖葫蘆

Word List

[1] braised [brezd] adj. 以文火燉煮的
[2] ginger [ˋdʒɪndʒɚ] n. 薑
[3] oyster [ˋɔɪstɚ] n. 牡蠣
[4] omelet [ˋɑmlɪt] n. 煎蛋餅；煎蛋捲
[5] vermicelli [ˌvɝməˋsɛlɪ] n. （義大利）細麵條
[6] steamed [stimd] adj. 蒸煮的
[7] stewed [stjud] adj. 燜的；燉的
[8] stinky [ˋstɪŋkɪ] adj. 臭的；發臭的

[9] boiled [bɔɪld] adj. 煮熟的；煮沸的
[10] glutinous [ˋglutɪnəs] adj. 黏稠的（glutinous rice 糯米）
[11] marinated [ˋmærəˌnetɪd] adj. 用滷汁浸泡過的
[12] pearl [pɝl] n. 珍珠
[13] gelatin [ˋdʒɛlətn] n. 動／植物膠

34 中式料理詞彙：台灣食物 II MP3 35
Chinese Food Vocabulary : Taiwanese Food II

傳統菜
- cold noodles 涼麵
- curry over rice 咖哩飯
- fried leek¹ dumpling 韭菜盒
- pork knuckle² 豬腳肉
- pork/chicken cutlet³ 炸豬排／炸雞排
- minced⁴ pork on rice 魯肉飯
- sesame oil chicken 麻油雞

- three cups chicken 三杯雞
- shredded⁵ chicken on rice 雞絲飯
- turkey rice bowl 火雞肉飯
- thick soup with cuttlefish⁶ 花枝羹
- shabu-shabu 涮涮鍋

夜市的食物
- barbequed squid⁷ 烤魷魚
- coffin⁸ bread 棺材板

- lumpia 潤餅
- Shawarma 沙威馬

甜點
- grass jelly 仙草
- suncake 太陽餅

- wheel cake 車輪餅

Part 4 食物和飲料

Word List

1 leek [lik] n. 韭菜
2 knuckle [`nʌk]] n. 踝關節或腕關節部分（的肉）
3 cutlet [`kʌtlɪt] n. 肉片；炸肉排
4 minced [mɪnst] adj. 剁碎的；絞碎的

5 shredded [`ʃrɛdɪd] adj. 切絲的；切成條狀的
6 cuttlefish [`kʌtl.fɪʃ] n. 花枝；墨魚；烏賊
7 squid [skwɪd] n. 魷魚
8 coffin [`kɔfɪn] n. 棺材

小吃
- congee[1] 粥
- dim sum 點心
- egg tart 蛋撻
- jelly dessert (guilinggao) 龜令膏
- phoenix[2] talons[3] (chicken feet) 鳳爪
- curry pastry[4] 咖哩酥餃
- rice noodle roll(s) 腸粉
- fried bun(s) （上海）生煎包
- roast pork bun(s) 叉燒包
- little basket bun(s) 小籠包
- chao-chiu style dumpling(s) 潮州粉果
- shrimp dumpling(s) 蝦餃

- spinach[5] steamed dumpling(s) 翡翠蒸餃
- steamed dumpling(s) 蒸餃
- steamed pork dumpling(s) (shaomai) 燒賣
- watercress[6] dumpling(s) 西菜餃
- sweet soup 甜湯
- black sesame soup 芝麻糊
- red/green bean soup 紅／綠豆湯
- taro[7] cake 芋頭糕
- coffee milk tea (yuanyang) 鴛鴦

Word List

[1] congee [ˋkɑndʒi] n. 粥
[2] phoenix [ˋfinɪks] n. 鳳凰
[3] talon [ˋtælən] n. （猛禽等的）爪
[4] pastry [ˋpestrɪ] n. 酥皮點心

[5] spinach [ˋspɪnɪtʃ] n. 菠菜
[6] watercress [ˋwɔtəˏkrɛs] n. 水田芥
[7] taro [ˋtɑro] n. 芋頭

傳統菜

- beef stew 燉牛肉
- beef with wide rice noodles 乾炒牛河
- braised crispy chicken 炸子雞
- seasoned[1] roast chicken 鹽焗雞
- soy sauce chicken 豉油雞
- soy sauce duck 滷水鴨
- roast goose 燒鵝
- pork ribs 豬肋排
- roast suckling[2] pork 烤乳豬
- spit-roasted[3] pork 叉燒肉
- salt and pepper fried squid/shrimp 椒鹽魷魚／蝦

- steamed/stir-fried fish intestines[4] 蒸／炒魚腸
- lo mein 撈麵
- meat and vegetables over rice 燴飯
- Buddha[5] jumps over the wall 佛跳牆
- three treasures rice 三寶飯
- abalone[6] soup 鮑魚煲湯
- bird's nest[7] soup 燕窩
- shark[8] fin[9] soup 魚翅煲湯
- wonton soup/noodles 雲吞湯／麵

Part 4 食物和飲料

Word List

[1] seasoned [ˈsiznd] adj. 調過味的
[2] suckling [ˈsʌklɪŋ] n. 不斷奶的；幼獸
[3] spit-roasted 用鐵叉烤的（spit [spɪt] n. 烤肉用的鐵叉子）
[4] intestine [ɪnˈtɛstɪn] n. 腸（常用複數）

[5] Buddha [ˈbudə] n. 佛陀；佛
[6] abalone [ˌæbəˈlonɪ] n. 鮑魚
[7] nest [nɛst] n. 鳥巢
[8] shark [ʃɑrk] n. 鯊魚
[9] fin [fɪn] n. 魚鰭

37 中式料理詞彙：中國北方食物
Chinese Food Vocabulary : Northern P.R.C. Food

小吃
- beef pie 牛肉餡餅
- beef roll 牛肉捲餅
- boiled dumpling(s) 水餃
- pot sticker(s) 鍋貼
- red chili[1] dumpling(s) 紅油抄手
- deep fried strip[2] (youtiao) 油條
- millet[3] porridge 小米粥
- roasted flatbread[4] with sesame seeds (shaobing) 芝麻燒餅

- scallion[5] pancake(s) 蔥油餅
- Shandong steamed bun(s) 山東饅頭
- steamed (pork/vegetable) bun(s) 肉包／菜包
- steamed bun with fried egg 饅頭夾蛋
- Tianjin "goubuli" steamed bun(s) 天津苟不理包子
- soy milk 豆漿

傳統菜
- Beijing roast duck 北京烤鴨
- hot and sour soup 酸辣湯
- soup noodles 湯麵

- beef noodle soup 牛肉麵
- knife-sliced[6] noodles 刀削麵
- savory[7] thick noodles 大滷麵

Word List

1 chili [ˋtʃɪlɪ] n. 紅辣椒
2 strip [strɪp] n. 細長的條
3 millet [ˋmɪlɪt] n. 小米
4 flatbread [ˋflæt͵brɛd] n. 大餅

5 scallion [ˋskæljən] n. 青蔥
6 knife-sliced 用刀削成薄片的 (slice [slaɪs] v. 切成薄片)
7 savory [ˋsevərɪ] adj. 鹹的；香辣的

38 中式料理詞彙：餐廳常見菜餚  MP3 39

Chinese Food Vocabulary : Typical Restaurant Dishes

統菜 ■ chow mein (stir-fried noodles) 炒麵

■ fried rice 炒飯

■ ants climbing a tree 螞蟻上樹

■ beef and scallions 蔥爆牛肉

■ iron plate tofu/beef/etc. 鐵板豆腐／牛肉／等等

■ kung-pao chicken 宮保雞丁

■ lion's head meatball(s) 紅燒獅子頭

■ mapo tofu 麻婆豆腐

■ stir-fried sliced potato 炒土豆絲

■ sweet and sour ribs/fish 糖醋排骨／魚

■ twice-cooked[1] pork 回鍋肉

■ yuxiang eggplant[2] 魚香茄子

Word List

1 twice-cooked 煮兩遍的
2 eggplant [ˋɛg͵plænt] *n.* 茄子

以下提供幾種如何形容食物和食物的大概料理方式。閱讀時，看看是否能猜得出描述的食物是什麼。

台灣 ☐ The pork cutlet is breaded, and then deep-fried.

先將豬肉片裹上麵包粉，然後油炸。

☐ The noodles are boiled and then stir-fried with meat and vegetables.

先將麵煮熟，然後放入肉和蔬菜一起炒。

北方 ☐ The meat and vegetable filling[1] is wrapped[2] in dough[3] and then boiled.

把肉和蔬菜餡料用麵團包好，然後煮熟。

☐ The ingredients[4] are cooked and brought to the table on a hot iron plate.

將煮過的食材放在燒燙的鐵盤上端上桌。

南方 ☐ The fish is steamed whole with spring onion,[5] ginger, and soy sauce.

整隻魚加青蔥、薑和醬油一起蒸。

☐ The dumplings are steamed and served in the steamer basket.

餃子蒸好之後，放在蒸籠裡端上桌。

Word List

[1] filling [ˋfɪlɪŋ] *n.* 內餡
[2] wrap [ræp] *v.* 包；裹
[3] dough [do] *n.* 麵團

[4] ingredient [ɪnˋgridɪənt] *n.* 烹飪食材
[5] spring onion 青蔥（= green onion）

40 描述料理方法（詳細說明） 🎧 MP3 41

Describing How Something Is Cooked (Specific)

這裡提供三種形容菜餚的詳細料理方法。你可以仿照這些句型為你的訪客描述其他菜餚的料理方法。

台灣 □ Zhajiang noodles are noodles topped with a sauce that is made by stir-frying ground[1] pork, tofu, green onions, and fish sauce. Sliced cucumbers[2] (and carrots) are then added.

炸醬麵是在麵條上面淋上用肉燥、豆腐、青蔥和海鮮醬炒好的醬汁，然後加上小黃瓜（和紅蘿蔔）絲。

北方 □ Kung-pao chicken is made from chopped, marinated chicken. The chicken is stir-fried with chopped green onions, garlic,[3] chili peppers, peanuts and soy sauce.

宮保雞丁是用剁碎並以滷汁醃過的雞肉做成的。把雞肉和切碎的青蔥、蒜頭、紅辣椒、花生和醬油放在一起炒。

南方 □ Phoenix talons are actually chicken feet that are deep-fried or boiled, marinated in a black bean sauce, and then steamed.

鳳爪其實就是經油炸、煮熟並用黑豆醬油滷過，之後再蒸的雞腳。

Part 4 食物和飲料

Word List

[1] ground [graʊnd] *adj.* 磨碎的
[2] cucumber [ˋkjukəmbə] *n.* 黃瓜
[3] garlic [ˋgɑrlɪk] *n.* 大蒜；蒜頭

41 提議吃什麼食物
Making Food Suggestions

☐ How about oil strip, porridge, and hot soymilk[1] for breakfast?

早餐吃油條、稀飯和熱豆漿如何？

☐ I think you'll like a dànbǐng. You can get plain,[2] bacon, ham, corn, or tuna.[3]

我想您會喜歡蛋餅的。您可以選擇原味、培根、火腿、玉米或鮪魚。

☐ We'll have biàndāng for lunch. It's a box with rice, vegetables, and choice of meat or fish

我們中午會吃便當。便當裡有飯、蔬菜，還可以選擇肉或是魚。

☐ Dànbāofàn is kind of fun. It's like an omelet filled with fried rice.

蛋包飯蠻有趣的。就像是煎蛋捲裡面包炒飯。

☐ It's kind of cold. Maybe we should think about shabu-shabu.

天氣有點冷。或許我們可以考慮吃涮涮鍋。

☐ There's nothing like shaved[4] ice on a hot night like this.

像今天晚上這麼熱，沒有比吃刨冰更好的了。

Word List

1 soymilk [ˋsɔɪ͵mɪlk] *n.* 豆漿
2 plain [plen] *adj.* 不含其他物質的；簡單平實的
3 tuna [ˋtunə] *n.* 鮪魚
4 shaved [ʃevd] *adj.* 刨的；削的

42 | 推薦吃什麼食物
Making Food Recommendations[1]

☐ I recommend[2] the special. It's what this place is known for.[3]

我推薦特餐。這個地方就是以這個出名的。

☐ I had the beef noodle soup the last time I was here. You can't go wrong.

我上一次來這裡就是吃牛肉湯麵。您選這個就對了。

☐ I know an ice cream shop that has sesame chicken flavor.[4] You've got to try it.

我知道有一家冰淇淋店有麻油雞口味的。您一定要試試看。

☐ If you're feeling like[5] something savory, go for the beef and tomato hùifàn.

如果您想吃口味重一點的，就吃番茄牛肉燴飯。

☐ I think you should try the oyster vermicelli. It's a classic dish.

我覺得您應該試試蚵仔麵線。這是道經典的小吃。

☐ If you're not too hungry, the cold noodles are a good choice.

如果您不是很餓，涼麵是個不錯的選擇。

Part 4

食物和飲料

Word List

1 recommendation [ˌrɛkəmɛnˋdeʃən] *n.* 推薦

2 recommend [ˌrɛkəˋmɛnd] *v.* 推薦；介紹

3 be known for... 以……而聞名

4 flavor [ˋflevə] *n.* 味道；風味

5 feel like 想要

43 點餐：菜單
Ordering : The Menu

□ Let me tell you what's on the menu.

我來告訴您菜單上有些什麼。

□ What looks good to you?

您覺得哪些菜色看起來不錯？

□ Get anything you'd like. Just point[1] to what looks interesting.

您想吃什麼就點什麼。只要指一下那些看起來好吃的就行了。

□ How about what that man over there is eating?

試試那邊那位男士在吃的東西如何？

□ I can order for you if you'd like.

如果您要的話，我可以幫您點餐。

□ This is a family-style place, so I'll just order a bunch[2] of dishes and we'll share.

這是一間家常菜餐館，所以我會點幾道菜，我們一起吃。

Word List

[1] point [pɔɪnt] v. 指；指向
[2] bunch [bʌntʃ] n. 一群；一串；一束

44 點餐：決定選項

🎧 MP3 45

Ordering : Choosing Among Alternatives[1]

食物 ☐ You can have the noodles dry, in soup, or stir-fried.

您可以吃乾麵、湯麵或者炒麵。

☐ How spicy would you like your curry?

您的咖哩要多辣？

☐ Would you like the set meal? It includes soup, salad, and a drink.

您想不想吃套餐？套餐包括湯、沙拉還有飲料。

飲料 ☐ Would you like coffee, tea, or juice?

您要喝咖啡、茶，還是果汁？

☐ You can have the coffee hot or iced.

您可以喝熱咖啡或冰咖啡。

☐ Would you like your drink now or with your meal?

您想要現在就上飲料，還是隨餐上？

Part 4 食物和飲料

■ alternative [ɔl`tɜnətɪv] *n.* 可供選擇的事物

Word List

45 形容滋味
Describing Flavor

☐ The soup is a little sour.

這湯有一點酸。

☐ If it tastes bland,[1] add some of this sauce. It's salty.

如果吃起來沒什麼味道，加些這個佐料。是鹹的。

☐ These dumplings have a sweet filling. Those are savory.

這些水餃的內餡是甜的。那些是鹹的。

☐ The fish is very fresh. Be careful with the bones.

這條魚很新鮮。小心魚刺。

☐ It tastes better than it smells.

這吃起來比聞起來好。

☐ Careful. The curry is temperature[2] hot, but it's not spicy.

小心。這咖哩有些燙，但是並不會辣。

Word List

1 bland [blænd] *adj.* 淡而無味的；無刺激性的
2 temperature [ˋtɛmprətʃə] *n.* 溫度

46 | 形容口感
Describing Texture[1]

☐ **The mochi is really chewy.[2]**

這麻薯很有嚼勁。

☐ **These rice noodles are very springy.[3]**

這些米粉很有彈性。

☐ **The outside is crispy and the inside is juicy.**

外面是脆的，裡面有汁。

☐ **The beef is tender[4] but the pork is a little tough.[5]**

這牛肉很嫩，但是豬肉有一點老。

☐ **The steamed vegetables are perfect: not too soft and not too crisp.**

這蒸過的蔬菜好吃極了：不會太軟也不會太脆。

☐ **The pudding is nice and creamy.**

這布丁好吃，很有奶油味。

Part 4

食物和飲料

Word List

1 texture [ˋtɛkstʃə] *n.* 組織；結構
2 chewy [ˋtʃuɪ] *adj.* 不易咀嚼的
3 springy [ˋsprɪŋɪ] *and.* 有彈性的

4 tender [ˋtɛndə] *adj.* 嫩的；柔軟的
5 tough [tʌf] *adj.* （肉）老的；堅韌的

47 甜點
Desserts

☐ The set meal includes dessert.

套餐包括甜點。

☐ You can choose cake, an egg tart, ice cream, or pudding.

您可以選擇蛋糕、蛋塔、冰淇淋，或者是布丁。

☐ It's a sweet soup made with peanuts. Try it.

這是用花生做成的甜湯。試試看。

☐ Pick any three toppings[1] for your shaved ice.

您可以任選三種料淋在刨冰上。

☐ The glutinous rice balls (tangyuan) are filled with sesame paste.[2]

這湯圓裡面包的是芝麻糊。

☐ This shop is famous for its wheel cakes (chelunbing). I like the cream filling.

這家店以車輪餅出名。我喜歡奶油餡的。

Word List

1 topping [ˋtɑpɪŋ] *n.* 淋在食物上的調味料
2 paste [pest] *n.* 糊狀物；醬；膏

48 餐館的氣氛
Atmosphere[1] of Eatery[2]

☐ I'm sorry, I didn't hear you. This place is kind of noisy.

對不起，我聽不見你說話。這地方蠻吵的。

☐ The interior[3] design in here is really interesting.

這裡面的室內裝潢很有意思。

☐ This is one of the classiest[4] places in town.

這是市區裡最有格調的餐館之一。

☐ These private banquet[5] rooms are cozy.[6]

這些隱密的宴會廳很舒適。

☐ This is a very typical[7] local restaurant.

這是間非常典型的本地餐館。

☐ It doesn't look like much, but the food is great.

這家店看起來不怎麼樣，但是東西很好吃。

Part 4 食物和飲料

 Word List

1 atmosphere [ˈætməsˌfɪr] *n.* 氣氛
2 eatery [ˈitərɪ] *n.* 餐館
3 interior [ɪnˈtɪrɪə] *adj.* 內部的
4 classy [ˈklæsɪ] *adj.* 高級的；有格調的

5 banquet [ˈbæŋkwɪt] *n.* 宴會；盛宴
6 cozy [ˈkozɪ] *adj.* 舒適的
7 typical [ˈtɪpɪkl] *adj.* 典型的

49 結帳：你作東
Paying the Bill : You Pay

 MP3 50

☐ It's my treat.[1]

我請客。

☐ I've got the bill. I'll let you get the next one.

帳單在我這兒。（我去結帳。）下一次再讓您請。

☐ Do you mind if we split[2] the bill?

您介不介意我們各付各的？

☐ We'll put it on my card.

我們用我的信用卡刷。

☐ This one is on the company.

這一頓公司出錢。

☐ In Chinese culture, it's common[3] for people to fight over paying the bill.

在中國文化裡，人們常常搶著付帳。

Word List

1 treat [trit] *n.* 請客
2 split [splɪt] *v.* 分開
3 common [`kɑmən] *adj.* 常見的；普通的

50 結帳：讓訪客作東

Paying the Bill : Have Your Guest Pay

MP3 51

☐ I'll let you get this one.
這一次就讓您請了。

☐ Do you mind picking up the tab?[1]
您介不介意這次讓您付錢？

☐ Oh, no! I don't have enough cash. Can you spot me?[2]
慘了！我帶的現金不夠。您可以借我錢嗎？

☐ You pay and we'll square up[3] later.
您先付錢，我們之後再算清楚。

☐ I can't believe it! I forgot my wallet. I'll pay you back.
我真不敢相信！我忘了帶錢包。我會還您錢的。

☐ Will you need a receipt for the meal?
您需要用餐的收據嗎？

Part 4 食物和飲料

Word List

1 tab [tæb] *n.* 帳單；費用
2 spot sb. 【口語】借錢給某人
3 square up 結清

51 飲料：在市區喝飲料時
Beverages[1] : Soft Drinks[2] While Out on the Town

☐ The tap water[3] is safe, but most people still drink bottled water.
喝自來水是安全的，但是大部分的人都喝瓶裝水。

☐ The convenience[4] stores sell all kinds of tea drinks.
便利商店販賣各式各樣的茶飲。

☐ They don't serve drinks so I'm going to get something from 7-11. What would you like?
他們不提供飲料，所以我打算去 7-11 買。您想喝什麼？

☐ Yogurt[5] drinks are pretty popular in the summer.
酵母乳飲料在夏天非常受歡迎。

☐ Have you ever had a papaya milk shake?[6]
您喝過木瓜牛奶嗎？

☐ Shaved-ice places also have lots of blended[7] fruit drinks.
刨冰店也賣很多種綜合果汁。

Word List

[1] beverage [ˋbɛvərɪdʒ] *n.* 飲料
[2] soft drink 不含酒精的飲料，如汽水
[3] tap water 自來水（tap [tæp] *n.* 水龍頭）
[4] convenience [kənˋvinjəns] store 便利商店
[5] yogurt [ˋjogət] *n.* 優格；酸乳酪；酵母乳
[6] milk shake [ˋmɪlk ˌʃek] *n.* 奶昔
[7] blended [ˋblɛndɪd] *adj.* 數種混和的

52 飲料：在市區喝其他飲料時 MP3 53

Beverages : Other Drinks While Out on the Town

☐ This cart has fresh squeezed[1] and blended drinks. What's your poison?[2]

這個推車攤販有新鮮現榨的綜合飲料。您想喝什麼？

☐ I'm feeling a little drowsy.[3] Want to get a cup of coffee with me?

我覺得有點睏。想不想和我一起去喝杯咖啡？

☐ This vendor is selling lemonade.

這個攤販在賣檸檬汁。

☐ The basements of the big department stores have grocery stores. You can get a nice bottle of wine there.

這家大型百貨公司的地下室有雜貨店。您可以到那兒買瓶好酒。

☐ Convenience stores have a decent[4] selection[5] of imported[6] and domestic[7] beer.

便利商店有許多優質的進口和國產啤酒可供您選購。

☐ You're looking for a bottle of tequila?[8] Let me find a place that sells spirits.[9]

您想買瓶龍舌蘭酒？我來幫您找家賣烈酒的店。

 Word List

1 squeezed [skwizd] *adj.* 榨的
2 What's your poison?
　　可用此句話來問對方想喝什麼。
3 drowsy [ˋdrauzɪ] *adj.* 昏昏欲睡的
4 decent [ˋdisn̩t] *adj.* 像樣的

5 selection [səˋlɛkʃən] *n.* 可供選購的同類物品
6 imported [ɪmˋportɪd] *adj.* 進口的
7 domestic [dəˋmɛstɪk] *adj.* 國內的
8 tequila [təˋkilə] *n.* 龍舌蘭酒
9 spirits [ˋspɪrɪts] *n.* （常作複數）烈酒

53 飲料：餐廳的茶和紅茶攤的茶 🎧 MP3 54

Beverages : Tea at a Restaurant and Tea Stand

餐廳 □ They have oolong, jasmine,[1] pu-erh, and green tea.
他們有烏龍茶、茉莉花茶、普洱茶，和綠茶。

□ Would you like milk tea, lemon tea, or an herbal[2] tea?
您想喝奶茶、檸檬茶、還是花草茶？

□ Let's let the tea steep[3] for a few more minutes.
我們讓茶再浸泡幾分鐘。

紅茶攤 □ You can't visit Taiwan without trying a pearl milk tea.
您到台灣來不能不試試珍珠奶茶。

□ They can make it with reduced[4] sugar if you prefer.
如果您比較喜歡，他們可以做少糖的。

□ I think you'd better use one of the thick straws.
我想您最好使用粗一點的吸管。

Word List

[1] jasmine [`dʒæsmɪn] *n.* 茉莉花
[2] herbal [`ɜbl] *adj.* 草本的
[3] steep [stip] *v.* 浸泡
[4] reduced [rɪ`djust] *adj.* 減少的；降低的

54 | 飲料：茶館的茶
Beverages : Tea at a Tea House

☐ If you like any of the teas we try, you can buy some to take home.

如果您喜歡任何我們喝過的茶，可以買一些帶回家。

☐ How are you with caffeine?[1] If it keeps you up,[2] I'll order herbal or flower tea.

您喝含咖啡因的飲料會有什麼影響嗎？如果喝了會讓您睡不著，我就會點花草茶或花茶。

☐ We always dump[3] out the first pot.

我們通常會把第一壺茶沖掉。

☐ The tea goes from the pot into this small pitcher[4] and then into these tall cups.[5]

把茶從茶壺倒入這個小壺裡，然後再倒入這些聞香杯中。

☐ Pour[6] the tea into the drinking cup and then smell the tall cup.

把茶倒入這只飲杯裡，然後聞聞這只聞香杯。

☐ When someone pours you a cup, you can knock on the table, like this, to say thanks.

如果有人為您倒了一杯茶，您可以像這樣敲敲桌子，表示謝意。

Word List

[1] caffeine [ˈkæfiɪn] *n.* 咖啡因
[2] keep sb. up 使某人睡不著
[3] dump [dʌmp] *v.* 傾倒

[4] pitcher [ˈpɪtʃə] *n.* 壺
[5] tall cup 聞香杯
[6] pour [por] *v.* 倒；灌

55 酒吧和夜店 I
Bars and Pubs I

邀請 ☐ How about going out for a drink?

出去喝杯酒如何？

☐ You up for a place where we can just chat,[1] or do you want to go somewhere a little more fun?

您想去我們可以純聊天的地方，還是去好玩一點的地方？

☐ We have lots of choices: a local karaoke bar, a standard[2] pub, or a place with lots of Westerners.[3]

我們有許多選擇：本地的卡拉 OK 店，一般的夜店，或有許多外國人的地方。

在酒吧 ☐ You feel like a beer or a cocktail?

您想喝啤酒還是雞尾酒？

☐ This place is kind of loud and smoky. Let's go somewhere else.

這地方有點吵，煙霧瀰漫。我們去別的地方吧。

☐ Care for[4] a game of pool[5] or darts?[6]

想打撞球或射飛鏢嗎？

Word List

1 chat [tʃæt] v. 開聊
2 standard [ˋstændəd] adj. 普通的；一般的
3 Westerner [ˋwɛstənə] n. 西方人；歐美人

4 care for 喜歡；想要
5 pool [pul] n. 撞球
6 dart [dɑrt] n. 飛鏢

56 酒吧和夜店 II
Bars and Pubs II

責任主
人時

☐ Care for a refill?[1] / How about another?

要不要再來一杯？／再來一杯如何？

☐ Let me get this round.[2]

這一輪我請。

☐ I think we should call it a night.[3]

我想我們今晚喝到這裡就好了。

敬酒時

☐ Cheers. Here's to our health.

乾杯。祝大家健康。

☐ Here's mud in your eye.[4]

乾杯！

☐ To toast.[5]

乾杯！

Part
4
食
物
和
飲
料

Word
List

[1] refill [ˋrifɪl] *n.* 添補物（此處指再把酒杯斟滿）
[2] round [raʊnd] *n.* （酒的）一巡；一輪
[3] call it a night 【口語】今晚到此結束

[4] Here's mud in your eye.
（口語）敬酒時可用此詞語。
[5] toast [tost] *v./n.* 舉杯祝酒

57 晚宴：基本事項
Banquet[1] Meal : Basics

MP3 58

安排 ☐ We'd like to invite you to attend our company's end-of-the-year banquet.[2]

我們想邀請您參加我們公司的尾牙。

☐ It will be held on Thursday evening at 7:00. We'll provide transportation.

晚宴將在星期四晚上七點舉行。我們會提供交通工具。

☐ It'll be semiformal,[3] so we'll have to stop by[4] the hotel to change first.

這會是半正式的場合，所以我們將得先回飯店一下換衣服。

用餐 ☐ Watch what I do. Serve others first, and then take a little for
當中　 yourself.

看我怎麼做。先為別人夾菜，然後再夾一點給自己。

☐ When you toast someone, hold the cup in both hands and say "gan bei."

當您要跟別人敬酒時，用雙手握住杯子，然後說「乾杯」。

☐ Can you please tell me why this is called a "lazy Susan"?[5]

能不能請您告訴我為什麼這個叫做 Lazy Susan ？

Word List

1 banquet [`bæŋkwɪt] *n.* 宴會
2 end-of-the-year banquet 尾牙
3 semiformal [ˌsɛmaɪ`fɔrml] *adj.* 半正式的
4 stop by （順道）作短暫停留
5 lazy Susan [`lezɪ `suzn̩] *n.* 餐桌中間的圓轉盤

58 晚宴：飲料
Banquet Meal : Beverages

☐ They'll probably serve orange juice, guava[1] juice, and Shaoxing wine.

他們可能會供應柳橙汁、芭樂汁，和紹興酒。

☐ I don't know why, but they always use small glasses at banquets.

我不知道為什麼宴會上都用小玻璃杯。

☐ They usually provide tea at the end of the meal, but I could order some now if you'd like.

通常在餐後會上茶，但是如果您想喝，我現在可以幫您點。

☐ Let me pour some beer for you.

我來幫您倒杯啤酒。

☐ Would you like to try some rice wine?

您要不要試試米酒？

☐ I'd like to propose[2] a toast to Mr. Smith.

我想向史密斯先生敬一杯酒。

Word List

1 guava [ˋgwɑvə] *n.* 番石榴
2 propose [prəˋpoz] *v.* 提議（祝酒）

Part 4 食物和飲料

59 商業午餐／晚餐
Business Lunch/Dinner

安排 ☐ Let's continue our discussion over lunch.

我們吃午餐時再繼續討論吧。

☐ The director has invited us to dinner tonight.

主管邀請我們今晚一起吃晚餐。

☐ You could bring a gift if you'd like. A bottle of wine or something like that would be fine.

如果您要的話，可以帶件禮物去。帶一瓶酒之類的就可以了。

用餐中 ☐ Why don't you sit here?

您怎麼不坐這裡？

☐ Just laugh whenever I laugh. He likes telling jokes.

我笑的時候跟著笑就可以了。他喜歡說笑話。

☐ The boss said that we should talk about anything except business. He wants us to enjoy ourselves.

老闆說我們什麼都可以談，就是不要談公事。他希望我們能夠享受一下。

60 街邊小吃

Street Food

☐ This stall[1] serves lǔwèi. You can pick what you want, then it's stewed in soy sauce.

這攤賣滷味。您挑選喜歡吃的，選好之後再放入醬油裡燉煮。

☐ The barbecued corn and roasted yams are worth[2] a try.

烤玉米和烤番薯值得一試。

☐ If you feel like a sandwich, let's try the shāwēimǎ (Shawarma). You can choose the meat and flavor.

如果您想吃三明治，我們試試沙威瑪。您可以選擇不同的肉類和口味。

☐ If you like spring rolls, the rùnbǐng (lumpia) are quite good. I'll help you pick the filling.

如果您喜歡春捲，潤餅很好吃。我會幫您挑選內餡。

☐ Let's get some fried buns. We can walk, talk, and eat.

咱們買一些水煎包，可以邊走、邊聊、邊吃。

☐ Take a seat and I'll order some food. We can split it.

選個位子，我來點餐。我們可以一起吃。

Word List

1 stall [stɔl] *n.* 攤位
2 worth [wɜθ] *adj.* 值得（做）

Part**5**

氣候和語言
Weather and Language

溫度 ☐ It's about twenty degrees Celsius.[1] That's almost seventy degrees Fahrenheit.[2]

氣溫大約是攝氏二十度，差不多有華式七十度。

☐ It's going to get up into the low thirties[3] today.

今天氣溫會升到三十一、二度。

炎熱 ☐ Hot enough for you?

對您而言夠熱嗎？（您很熱吧？）

☐ The humidity[4] is what makes it feel so hot.

因為濕氣重所以會覺得特別熱。

寒冷 ☐ The winters here are really cold and damp.[5]

這裡的冬天真的是又濕又冷。

☐ Are you going to be warm enough? It's pretty chilly[6] outside.

您這樣真的夠暖和了嗎？外面很冷。

---

[1] Celsius [ˈsɛlsɪəs] n. 攝氏
[2] Fahrenheit [ˈfærənˌhaɪt] n. 華式
[3] the low thirties 三十一、二度
[4] humidity [hjuˈmɪdətɪ] n. 濕氣；濕度
[5] damp [dæmp] adj. 潮濕的
[6] chilly [ˈtʃɪlɪ] adj. 寒冷的

62 天氣：預測和建議
Weather : Forecasts[1] and Suggestions

☐ It might cool off[2] tonight, so I'd take a jacket.
今天晚上可能會變涼，所以我要帶件外套。

☐ It's going to be clear[3] tomorrow.
明天天氣會變晴朗。

☐ It might rain tomorrow afternoon, so bring an umbrella.
明天下午可能會下雨，所以最好帶把傘。

☐ The news said we might get some snow in the mountains.
新聞報導說山上可能會下雪。

☐ It's going to be hot tomorrow, so everyone needs to drink plenty
of water.
明天會很熱，所以大家須要多喝水。

☐ If there's a typhoon, we'll have to stay indoors.
如果明天颱風來襲，我們就得待在室內。

Part
5
氣候和語言

Word
List
1 forecast [ˈforˌkæst] n. 預測
2 cool off 變涼
3 clear [klɪr] adj. 晴朗的

討論國語：翻譯別人說的話

Talking about Mandarin[1] : Translating[2] What Others Are Saying

☐ **She's asking if you can take spicy food or not.**
她在問您能不能吃辣。

☐ **She said you're really good at[3] using chopsticks.[4]**
她說您真的很會用筷子。

☐ **She really likes your skirt.**
她很喜歡您的裙子。

☐ **He wants to know if you like it here.**
他想知道您喜不喜歡這裡。

☐ **Believe me, you don't want to know what they're saying.**
相信我，您絕對不會想知道他們在說些什麼。

☐ **Actually, that's not Mandarin. They're speaking Taiwanese.**
其實他們說的不是國語。他們說的是台語。

Word List

1 Mandarin [ˋmændərɪn] n.
國語；中國官方語言
2 translate [trænsˋlet] v. 翻譯

3 good at sth./Ving 善於做某事
4 chopsticks [ˋtʃɑpˏstɪks] n. 【複數型】筷子

64 討論國語：教人說基本的國語  MP3 65

Talking about Mandarin : Teaching Basic Mandarin Phrases

☐ A: How do you say "good night" in Chinese? B: Like this: "Wǎn ān."
　　A：「good night」的中文該怎麼說？ B：這樣說：「晚安」。

☐ "Good morning" is "zǎo."
　　Good morning 就是「早」。

☐ To say, "It's raining," you should say "xià yǔ le."
　　要說「It's raining.」您就說「下雨了。」

☐ When you're full you should say "wǒ chī bǎo le."
　　您吃飽的時候應該說：「我吃飽了。」

☐ You should know how to say hello: "Nǐ hǎo."
　　您應該知道如何打招呼：「你好」。

☐ You need to learn this one. "Thank you" is "xiè xiè."
　　您必須學會說這個。「Thank you」就是「謝謝」。

65 討論國語：聲調和國字

MP3 66

Talking about Mandarin : Tones[1] and Characters[2]

語調 ☐ Chinese is a tonal[3] language, which makes it kind of hard to learn.

中文是每個字都有聲調的語言，所以不太容易學。

☐ Mandarin has four tones. So, "mā", "má", "mǎ", and "mà" are all different words.

國語有四聲，所以「mā」、「má」、「mǎ」、「mà」是四個不同的字。

☐ 「媽」means "mother"; 「麻」means "hemp"; a 「馬」is a "horse"; and 「罵」means "to scold".[4]

國字 ☐ Most Chinese characters have two parts. The part that usually indicates the meaning of the character is called the radical.[5] The other part usually tells you how to pronounce[6] it.

大多數的國字都由兩個部分所組成。通常用來指出國字意義的部分叫做部首，另一部分通常告訴你如何發音。

☐ 「言」is the "speech" radical, so words related to[7] language often use 「言」. For example, 「詩」means "poetry", 「說」means "speak", and 「讀」means "to read". 「明」has a "sun" on the left, and a "moon" on the right. It means "bright".

「言」是表示「說話」的部首，所以和語言相關的字通常會是「言」部。舉例來說，「詩」就是「poetry」，「說」就是「speak」，「讀」就是「read」。「明」的左邊有個「日」，右邊有個「月」。它的意思是「明亮」。

Word List

1 tone [ton] n. 聲調
2 character [ˋkærəktə] n.（漢）字；字體
3 tonal [ˋtonl] adj. 有聲調的
4 scold [skold] v. 罵；斥責
5 radical [ˋrædɪkl] n. 部首
6 pronounce [prəˋnauns] v. 發音
7 relate to... 與……有關

66 討論國語：全世界的華人

Talking about Mandarin : Chinese in the World

MP3 67

☐ There are more than a billion[1] Mandarin speakers in the world today.

目前全世界說國語的人口超過十億。

☐ Most people in Taiwan can speak at least[2] two dialects.[3]

大說數的台灣人至少會說兩種語言。

☐ I speak Mandarin, Taiwanese, Hakka, and a little English.

我會說國語、台語、客家語，和一點英語。

☐ Actually, people in my grandparents' generation[4] speak Japanese fluently.[5]

事實上，我祖父、母那一輩的人日語說得很流利。

☐ I can't understand Cantonese at all.[6]

我對廣東話一竅不通。

☐ I heard that Mandarin is starting to get pretty popular in the U.S.

我聽說國語在美國開始變得很受歡迎。

Part 5
氣候和語言

Word List

1 billion [ˋbɪljən] n. 十億
2 at least 至少
3 dialect [ˋdaɪəlɛkt] n. 方言

4 generation [ˌdʒɛnəˋreʃən] n. 世代
5 fluently [ˋfluəntlɪ] adv. 流利地；流暢地
6 not at all 一點也不

Part**6**

觀光、活動、娛樂
Sightseeing, Activities, and Entertainment

67 博物館：運籌
Museum : Logistics

□ Wait here for just a minute while I get the tickets.
在這裡等一下，我去買票。

□ Let's take a look at[1] the map and decide where to go first.
咱們看一下地圖決定先去哪裡。

□ What I like about this place is the air conditioning[2] during the summer.
我之所以喜歡這個地方，是因為夏天有空調。

□ Let me see if they have an English-speaking guide.
我問一下這裡是否有英語導覽員。

□ There's a tea shop upstairs if you feel like sitting down.
如果您想坐下來休息一下，樓上有間茶館。

□ Let's meet back here at 3:30.
我們三點半回到這裡集合。

Word List

1 take a look at 看一下
2 air conditioning [ˈɛrkən͵dɪʃənɪŋ] n. 冷氣

68

博物館：評論藝術
Museum : Commenting[1] on Art

🎧 **MP3** 69

☐ This place has a good collection of traditional and contemporary[2] art.

這地方收藏了一些不錯的傳統和當代藝術作品。

☐ Ooo... That would look nice in my living room.

喔……那件作品如果放在我的客廳會蠻好看的。

☐ I really (don't) like the colors. What do you think?

我實在（不）喜歡這些顏色。您認為呢？

☐ What a piece of crap.[3] I could do better than that!

根本是件垃圾作品。我可以做比那更好的！

☐ Have you ever thought about quitting your job and becoming an artist?

您有沒有想過辭掉工作，成為一名藝術家？

☐ Well, it's like they say, "Life imitates[4] art." I think that's what this piece means.

嗯……這就像有句話說的：「生活模仿藝術」。我想那就是這件作品所要傳達的。

---

1 comment [ˋkɑmɛnt] v. 評論；批評
2 contemporary [kənˋtɛmpəˌrɛrɪ] adj. 當代的

3 crap [kræp] n. 廢物；屎
4 imitate [ˋɪməˌtet] v. 模仿；仿效

Word
List

69 藝術展覽
Art Exhibits[1]

☐ There's an interesting exhibit at a gallery nearby that I'd like to take you to.

附近一個美術館有個有趣的展覽，我想帶您去參觀。

☐ It's a display[2] of all local artists that includes photography,[3] sculpture,[4] and mixed media.[5]

裡面展示所有本地藝術家的作品，包括攝影、雕刻和複合媒材作品。

☐ My friend is hosting a gallery opening on Friday. Let me know if you'd like to go.

我的朋友星期五將會主持一間藝廊的開幕儀式。如果您想去可以告訴我。

☐ They may serve wine, but it's probably better to get something to eat first.

他們可能會提供酒，但是或許先吃一點東西比較好。

☐ This piece was done by an up-and-coming[6] local artist.

這件作品是由一位前途看好的本土藝術家所完成的。

☐ I don't know what it means, but kind of like it.

我不知道這件作品的意涵，但是還蠻喜歡的。

Word List

1 exhibit [ɪgˋzɪbɪt] n. 展覽；展品
2 display [dɪˋsple] n. 展覽；陳列
3 photography [fəˋtɑgrəfɪ] n. 攝影；攝影術
4 sculpture [ˋskʌlptʃə] n. 雕刻品；雕像
5 mixed media 用多種材質或方法完成的作品
6 up-and-coming 進取的；有前途的

70 本土藝術
Local Arts

 MP3 71

☐ If you have time, I'd like to take you to a Chinese opera on Monday night.

如果您有時間，星期一晚上我想帶您去看一場京劇。

☐ I think you'd enjoy seeing some aboriginal[1] dancing. There's a performance this evening.

我想您會喜歡看一些原住民舞蹈。今天晚上有一場表演。

☐ The Lantern Festival[2] display is really worth seeing. You've come at the right time of year.

元宵節的花燈真的很有看頭。一年中您來對時間了。

☐ After the meeting, we can check out[3] a calligraphy[4] exhibition.

會議結束之後，我們可以去看一場書法展。

☐ There's a town nearby famous for its pottery.[5] Would you like to check it out?

這附近有個小鎮以陶瓷聞名。您想不想去看看？

☐ Would you like to have a seal[6] made with your Chinese name?

您想不想要一個刻有您中文名字的印章？

Word List

1 aboriginal [ˌæbəˈrɪdʒənl] adj. 原始的；土著的
2 Lantern Festival [ˈlæntənˈfɛstəvl] 元宵節
3 check out【口語】瞧瞧；看看

4 calligraphy [kəˈlɪgrəfɪ] n. 書法
5 pottery [ˈpɑtərɪ] n. 陶器
6 seal [sil] n. 印章

 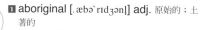

71 歷史古蹟
Historic Buildings

☐ This building dates[1] back to the Qing Dynasty,[2] which lasted[3] from 1644 to 1911.

這棟建築物建於清朝。清朝從西元 1644 年開始，1911 年結束。

☐ This stone tablet[4] explains when this place was built, who built it, and why.

這塊石碑說明這個地方的興建時間、興建人和興建的動機。

☐ The pillar[5]-and-beam[6] construction you see is very earthquake-resistant.[7]

您看到的樑柱結構防震功能很好。

☐ The Japanese built the Presidential Palace.[8] It opened in 1919.

現今的總統府是日本人興建的，於 1919 年開始啟用。

☐ There used to be a wall surrounding the city. This gate is all that's left of it.

這個城市以前有圍牆環繞，如今只剩下這座城門。

☐ We can look to the past to understand the present.

我們可以從過去瞭解現在。

Word List

1 date [det] v. 定年代
2 dynasty [ˋdaɪnəstɪ] n. 朝代；王朝
3 last [læst] v. 持續
4 tablet [ˋtæblɪt] n. 匾；碑
5 pillar [ˋpɪlə] n. 柱子

6 beam [bim] n. 橫樑
7 earthquake-resistant
　　[ˋɜθ͵kwɛk rɪˋzɪstənt] adj. 抗地震的
8 palace [ˋpælɪs] n. 宮殿（Presidential Palace 指總統府）

72 寺廟
Temples

☐ This is a Confucian/[1]Daoist/[2]Buddhist[3] temple.

這是一間孔子廟／道觀／佛寺。

☐ People come here to ask the gods for guidance when making a big decision.

當人們需要下重大決定時，會來此求神問卜。

☐ Let me show you what to do. Just follow my lead.[4]

我來教您怎麼做。只要跟著我做就行了。

☐ Hold the incense[5] like this, bow[6] three times, and then stick it in the burner.[7]

像這樣持香，鞠躬三次，然後把香插在香爐內。

☐ Let's cast[8] lots.[9] Make a wish and throw them on the ground.

我們來擲筊。許個願然後把筊丟在地上。

☐ One up and one down means "yes." Two down means "can't tell." Two up means "no."

一正一反表示「許可」。二反表示「不知道」。二正表示「不行」。

Word
List

[1] Confucian [kən`fjuʃən] adj. 孔子的
[2] Daoist [`dauɪst] adj. 道教的
[3] Buddhist [`budɪst] adj. 佛教的
[4] lead [lid] n. 指導；榜樣
[5] incense [`ɪnsɛns] n. 香

[6] bow [bau] v. 鞠躬
[7] burner [`bɜnɚ] n. 香爐
[8] cast [kæst] v. 投；擲
[9] lot [lɑt] n. 籤（cast lots 指擲筊）

73 公園
Parks

☐ Those people are practicing tai chi. Want to join them?

這些人正在打太極拳。想要加入他們嗎？

☐ Take your shoes off[1] and try walking on the stone path.[2]

脫掉您的鞋子，試試在這條石頭步道上走走。

☐ If this part of your foot hurts, that means something is wrong with your liver.[3]

如果您的腳這部分會痛，就表示您的肝有問題。

☐ I brought some bread to feed the koi[4] in the pond.

我買了一些麵包來餵池塘裡的鯉魚。

☐ This looks like a good spot for a picnic.

此處看起來像是個野餐的好地方。

☐ Care for a drink? There's a vending machine[5] over there.

想喝東西嗎？那邊有部自動販賣機。

Word List

[1] take sth. off 脫掉某物
[2] path [pæθ] n. 小徑；小路
[3] liver [ˈlɪvə] n. 肝臟
[4] koi [kɔɪ] n. 錦鯉
[5] vending machine [ˈvɛndɪŋ ˌməʃin] n. 自動販賣機

74 走向大自然
Natural Areas

出發
之前 ☐ Bring a jacket and be sure to wear comfortable shoes.

帶一件外套，而且一定要穿舒適的鞋子。

☐ You can bring a bathing suit[1] if you'd like. There's a small swimming hole there.

您要的話，可以帶件泳衣。那裡有個小型的泳洞。

☐ It's a four-hour hike[2] round trip.

這是一趟往返要四小時的徒步旅程。

目的地 ☐ I come here to get away from the rat race.[3]

我來這裡的目的是想遠離忙碌的工作生活。

☐ The view is really nice from up here.

從這高處看到的景色真的很棒。

☐ What are the national parks in your country like?

你們國家的國家公園是什麼樣子？

Word
List

[1] bathing suit [ˈbeðɪŋ ˌsut] n. 游泳衣；泳裝
[2] hike [haɪk] n. 健行；徒步旅行

[3] rat race n. （尤指商界）永無止境的競爭；
（都市工作生活的）勞碌奔波

75 攝影：擺姿勢

Photography : Posing[1] for Pictures

🎧 **MP3** 76

☐ Would you like me to get a picture for you?

您要不要我幫您拍張照？

☐ Let's take a picture together.

我們合照一張吧。

☐ Could you get a picture of me with that garden in the background?

您可不可以幫我拍一張照片，以後面的花園當背景？

☐ How does the flash[2] work on this thing?

這部相機的閃光燈怎麼操作？

☐ Move over there because there is more light.

往那邊移動，因為那裡光線比較充足。

☐ OK, on three. One... two... Ms. Smith, lean[3] to the left... three!

好，數到三。一、二、……史密斯女士，往左靠……三！

Word List

1 pose [poz] v. 擺姿勢
2 flash [flæʃ] n. 閃光；鎂光
3 lean [lin] v. 靠；傾身

76 攝影：關於照相機

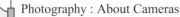

Photography : About Cameras

🎧 **MP3** 77

☐ Nice camera. How do you like it?

這部相機不錯。您覺得怎麼樣？

☐ How many megapixels[1] is that thing?

那部相機是幾百萬畫素的？

☐ How do you move the pictures from the camera to a computer?

您要怎麼把相機的照片傳輸到電腦？

☐ Can your camera film video clips?[2]

您的相機可以拍攝影片嗎？

☐ The image stabilization[3] on this one is great, but the battery life isn't.

這部相機的影像穩定度很棒，但是電池壽命則不然。

☐ This camera has fifty-six megs[4] (56MB) of internal[5] memory.

這部相機的內建記憶體容量是 56MB。

Word List

1 megapixel [ˋmɛgəˏpɪksəl] n. 百萬畫素
2 clip [klɪp] n.（影片）剪輯
3 stabilization [ˏstebləˋzeʃən] n. 穩定

4 meg [mɛg] n. 百萬位元（簡稱 MB）
5 internal [ɪnˋtɝnl] adj. 內部的

☐ Have you ever been to a night market? It's crowed, but totally safe.

您以前去過夜市嗎？夜市很擁擠，但是非常安全。

☐ If we get separated, let's meet back here (at 9:00).

我們如果走散了，（九點）回到這裡碰面。

☐ This place is great for people watching, if you're into[1] that.

如果您有興趣的話，這是個看人的好地方。

☐ Let's get a milk tea while we browse[2] around.

我們買杯奶茶一邊閒逛。

☐ How about getting some "big-head picture stickers"? They'll be a great souvenir.[3]

去照幾張大頭貼如何？會是很好的紀念品。

☐ Wow. Look at that line. The food at this stall must be really good.

哇！瞧那排隊伍。這個攤位的食物一定很好吃。

Word List

1 be into sth. 【口語】對……有興趣；熱衷於……
2 browse [braʊz] v. 隨意觀看；瀏覽
3 souvenir [ˋsuvəˌnɪr] n. 紀念品；土產

78 夜市：購物

Night Markets : Shopping

 MP3 79

關於更多的購物用語，請參閱第七章的購物篇。

☐ Are you looking for anything in particular?[1] Maybe I can help you find it.

您在找什麼特別的東西嗎？或許我可以幫您找。

☐ Let me know if you see anything you want to buy. I'll help you bargain.[2]

如果您看到什麼東西想買的就告訴我。我會幫你殺價。

☐ That lady is a fortuneteller.[3] Do you want to have your palm read?

這位女士是算命師。您想不想看手相？

☐ This waving[4] cat is supposed to[5] bring money into the shop. It's a good-luck thing.

這隻在招手的貓被認為會幫店家招來財富，是個吉祥物。

☐ When the police come, the vendors[6] without permits[7] have to move.

警察來的時候，沒有執照的攤販就必須離開。

☐ There are some shops where you just can't bargain, but it never hurts to ask.[8]

有些店家是沒辦法殺價的，但是問問無妨。

Word List

[1] in particular 特別；尤其
[2] bargain [ˋbɑrgən] v. 討價還價
[3] fortuneteller [ˋfɔrtʃən,tɛlə] n. 算命者
[4] wave [wev] v. 揮手

[5] be supposed to 被認為必須要；應該
[6] vendor [ˋvɛndə] n. 小販
[7] permit [ˋpɝmɪt] n. 許可證；執照
[8] It never hurts to v. 做……無傷。

泡湯：出發前
Hot Springs :[1] Before You Go

🎧 MP3 80

☐ Most places have a communal[2] area and also private rooms.

大部分的地方都有一個公共浴池也有私人浴池。

☐ Most of the communal areas are mixed, so you usually have to wear a bathing suit.

大多數的公共浴池不分男女，所以人們通常必須穿泳衣。

☐ Don't worry. They sell cheap swimsuits and bathing caps there.

不用擔心，他們那邊有賣便宜的泳衣和泳帽。

☐ Water and towels are always provided.

通常會供應水和毛巾。

☐ Some are indoor and some are outdoor. And some places have patios[3] with really nice views.

有些是室內池，有些是室外池。而有些地方有庭院，景色非常好。

☐ Don't eat too much because the place we're going also serves pretty good food.

不要吃太多，因為我們要去的地方也提供美食。

Word List
1 hot spring [`hɑt`sprɪŋ] n. 溫泉
2 communal [`kɑmjʊnl] adj. 公共的；共有的
3 patio [`pɑtɪ‚o] n. 庭院；中庭

80 泡湯：抵達湯池

MP3 81

Hot Springs : At the Hot Spring

□ OK, we change into our bathing suits here.

好，我們在這裡換泳衣。

□ Put your stuff in a locker[1] and take the key with you.

把您的東西放進儲物櫃裡，鑰匙要帶在身上。

□ We have to take a shower[2] first before we go in.

進池前我們必須先沖澡。

□ Careful. This pool is really hot.

小心。這池水很燙。

□ Push that button and see what happens.

按下那個開關，看看會怎麼樣。

□ You can dry off and relax a little in the dry sauna.[3]

您可以把身體擦乾，然後在蒸氣室放鬆一下。

Word List

[1] locker [`lɑkə] n. 儲物櫃
[2] take a shower 沖澡
[3] dry sauna [`draɪ`saʊnə] n. 蒸氣室

☐ Traditional holidays are based on[1] the lunar[2] calendar.
傳統節日是根據農曆制定的。

☐ The Lantern Festival falls on the fifteenth day of the first lunar month. We'll eat some glutinous rice balls (tangyuan).
元宵節是農曆第一個月的第十五天。我們會吃一些湯圓。

☐ Zongzi are the special food for the Dragon Boat Festival.[4]
粽子是端午節的應景食物。

☐ Most people don't get married or buy houses during Ghost Month.
大多數的人在鬼月不結婚、不買房子。

☐ Chinese New Year falls[5] in January or February.
中國新年逢一月或是二月。

Word List

[1] base on... 根據……
[2] lunar [ˈlunə] adj. 陰曆的；農曆的
[3] Mid-Autumn Festival 中秋節（autumn [ˈɔtəm] n. 秋天）

[4] Dragon Boat Festival 端午節（dragon boat [ˈdrægən ˌbot] n. 龍舟）
[5] fall [fɔl] v. 逢

82 本地的活動慶典 II
Local Events and Celebrations II

 MP3 83

☐ People set off[1] firecrackers[2] and fireworks[3] during the Spring Festival.

人們在春節期間施放鞭炮和煙火。

☐ Tomb Sweeping Day[4] is in April. We visit the graves[5] of our relatives.

清明節在四月。我們都會到親戚的墳墓去祭拜。

☐ Burning spirit money[6] and putting out offerings[7] is called baibai.

焚燒紙錢並擺出貢品叫做「拜拜」。

☐ Chinese Valentine's day[8] happens in August. Do you know the story of the Cowherder and the Weaver?

中國情人節在八月。你知道牛郎織女的故事嗎？

☐ Mid-Autumn Festival is celebrated in mid or late September each year, and everyone eats moon cakes on that day.

中秋節是在每年九月月中或月底的時候，那一天每個人都會吃月餅。

Word List

1 set off 施放
2 firecracker [ˋfaɪr͵krækɚ] n. 鞭炮；爆竹
3 fireworks [ˋfaɪr͵wɜks] n.【複數型】煙火
4 Tomb Sweeping Day 清明節（tomb [tum] n. 墳墓； sweep [swip] v. 掃）

5 grave [grev] n. 墳墓；墓地
6 spirit money 紙錢（spirit [ˋspɪrɪt] n. 靈魂）
7 offering [ˋɔfərɪŋ] n. 祭品；捐獻物
8 Valentine's [ˋvæləntaɪnz] Day 情人節

☐ Would you be interested in seeing a baseball game? I can get tickets.

您有沒有興趣看場棒球賽？我可以去買票。

☐ Would you like to see a martial arts[1] exhibition?[2]

您想不想看武術表演？

☐ If we get to the park early enough, we can see some people practicing the long sword.[3]

如果我們夠早到公園去，會看到一些練長劍的人。

☐ Are you following[4] the NBA playoffs?[5]

您有沒有在密切注意 NBA 決賽？

☐ I think your hotel room should have satellite[6] TV.

我想您的飯店應該有衛星電視。

☐ I know a sports bar[7] where we could watch the World Cup.[8]

我知道有家運動酒吧，我們可以在那裡看世界盃足球賽。

Word List

[1] martial arts 武術（martial [ˋmɑrʃəl] adj. 尚武的；好戰的）
[2] exhibition [ˌɛksəˋbɪʃən] n. 展示；展覽會
[3] sword [sord] n. 劍；刀

[4] follow [ˋfɑlo] v. 密切注意
[5] playoff [ˋpleˌɔf] n. 決賽
[6] satellite [ˋsætlˌaɪt] n. 衛星；人造衛星
[7] sports bar [ˋsportsˌbɑr] n. 運動酒吧
[8] World Cup 世界盃（足球賽）

84 運動：做運動
Sports : Playing

和你的訪客走到戶外去運動，是進一步認識對方的好方法，也有助於合作關係更加融洽。

☐ Do you play golf? My boss would like to take you to play a round.[1]
您打高爾夫球嗎？我的老闆想帶您去打一局。

☐ How about we go to a driving range[2] tonight and hit some balls?
我們今晚去高爾夫練習場打幾球如何？

☐ I'm not very good, but if you'd like to play a little tennis I could reserve[3] a court[4] for us.
我不太會打網球，但是如果您想要打，我可以去訂場地。

☐ Do you like basketball? Want to shoot some hoops?[5]
您喜歡打籃球嗎？想去投幾球嗎？

☐ Billiards[6] is pretty popular here. Care to shoot some pool?[7]
這裡非常流行打撞球。想不想去打幾桿？

☐ A few of us in the office go bowling[8] on Fridays. Would you like to come?
我們辦公室有幾個人星期五要去打保齡球。您要不要一起去？

Word List

[1] round [raʊnd] n.（高爾夫球賽中的）一局
[2] driving range [ˈdraɪvɪŋ ˌrendʒ] n. 高爾夫球練習場（drive 在此指擊球）
[3] reserve [rɪˈzɝv] v. 預約；預訂
[4] court [kort] n.（網球、籃球等的）場地

[5] shoot hoops 投籃（hoop [hup] n.（籃球的）籃圈）
[6] billiards [ˈbɪljədz] n.【複數型】撞球
[7] shoot pool 打撞球（pool [pul] n. 撞球）
[8] go bowling 去打保齡球（bowl [bol] v. 打保齡球）

☐ There should be some exercise equipment[2] in your hotel.

您的飯店應該有一些運動設施。

☐ If you're interested in working out,[3] I have a guest pass[4] for my gym.

如果您對健身感興趣，我去的健身房有張招待證。

☐ It has all kinds of classes and a full weight room.[5]

裡面有各式各樣的課程，還有設備齊全的舉重室。

☐ There's a track[6] on the east side of campus[7] where you can run some laps.[8]

校園的東側有跑道，您可以去跑幾圈。

☐ There are some hills just outside of town that are great for jogging.

市郊近區有一些小山丘，非常適合慢跑。

☐ Because of all the air pollution,[9] it's probably best to run early in the morning or late at night.

因為有空氣污染，所以清晨或深夜去跑步可能比較好。

Word List

[1] gym [dʒɪm] n. 健身房；體育館
（為 gymnasium [dʒɪm`nezɪəm] 的縮寫）

[2] equipment [ɪ`kwɪpmənt] n. 設備；裝備

[3] work out 健身

[4] guess pass 招待（入場）證

[5] weight room 有各種健身器材的舉重室

[6] track [træk] n. 跑道；小道

[7] campus [`kæmpəs] n. 校園

[8] lap [læp] n.（競賽場的）一圈；（游泳池的）來回；（旅程的）一段

[9] pollution [pə`luʃən] n. 污染

86 戶外活動
Outdoor Activities

MP3 87

□ Are you into any outdoor activities? I can help you arrange what you'd like to do.

您對戶外活動有興趣嗎？如果您想做什麼運動，我可以幫您安排。

□ If you want to go swimming, I could help locate[1] a good pool for you.

如果您想去游泳，我可以幫您找一家好的游泳池。

□ There are several rock climbing[2] walls around. I'll look into rental[3] equipment.

這附近有幾處不錯的攀岩牆。我會去找出租裝備。

□ I know a nice bike trail[4] along the river. If you're interested, we could rent bikes this weekend.

我知道沿河岸有條不錯的自行車道。如果您感興趣，這個週末我們可以去租腳踏車。

□ Kenting is a great place for scuba diving[5] and snorkeling.[6]

墾丁是潛水和浮潛的好去處。

□ You want to go fishing? I think I know someone you could go with.

您想去釣魚嗎？我想我認識一個人，您可以跟他一起去。

Word List

1 locate [lo`ket] v. 找出；探出
2 rock climbing [`rɑk.klaɪmɪŋ] n. 攀岩
3 rental [`rɛntl] adj. 供出租的
4 trail [trel] n. 小道
5 scuba diving [`skubə.daɪvɪŋ] n. 水肺潛水；帶氧氣筒潛水
6 snorkeling [`snɔrklɪŋ] n. 浮潛

87 電影
Movies

MP3 88

☐ Care to take in a movie?[1] It's a great way to beat[2] the heat.
想去看場電影嗎？這是個避暑的好方法。

☐ Interested in seeing a movie tomorrow night? I have free passes.
明天晚上有沒有興趣看一場電影？我有免費入場券。

☐ Want to see a local film, a Hollywood movie, or maybe something kind of arty?[3]
您想看本土電影、好萊塢電影，還是稍微藝術一點的電影？

☐ There's a pretty good Hong Kong cop[4] movie showing.
有一部蠻好看的香港警探片正上映中。

☐ The movies here are almost always subtitled[5] in English.
這裡的電影幾乎都有英語字幕。

☐ Most people here buy snacks outside the theater and bring them in.
這裡大多數的人都在戲院外面買零食，然後帶進去。

Word List

[1] take in a movie 看場電影
[2] beat [bit] v. 打敗；勝過；超越
[3] arty [`ɑrtɪ] adj. 故作藝術性的；附庸風雅的
[4] cop [kɑp] n. 【口語】警察
[5] subtitled [`sʌb.taɪt!d] adj. 有字幕的

88 表演
Performances

☐ There will be some plays at the National Theater[1] while you're here. Here's the program.

在您停留的這段期間，國家劇院有一些戲碼上演。這個是節目單。

☐ I have tickets to a modern dance performance Friday night. Will you be free?

我有星期五晚上現代舞蹈表演的票。您有空嗎？

☐ This dance troupe[2] is the best in the country. They perform abroad several times a year.

這個舞蹈團體是國內最優秀的。他們每年都會到國外作幾場表演。

☐ Some students are screening[3] their film projects[4] at the university. Could be interesting.

有些學生正在這所大學放映他們的電影作業。可能會很有趣。

☐ I've made arrangements to take you to see a Chinese opera Tuesday night.

我已經安排好星期二晚上帶您去看京劇。

☐ Did you enjoy the performance? What was your favorite part?

您喜歡這場表演嗎？您最喜歡哪一段？

Word List

1 National Theater [ˈθiətɚ] 國家劇院
2 troupe [trup] n.（演員等的）一團；一班
3 screen [skrin] v. 放映

4 project [ˈprɑdʒɛkt] n. 企劃；方案；大型作業

演唱會和現場音樂演奏
Concerts and Live Music

☐ If you like classical music, I can take you to the symphony.[1]

如果您喜歡古典樂，我可以帶您去聽交響樂。

☐ While you're here, we should check out some traditional Chinese music.

在您停留的這段期間，我們應該去欣賞一些傳統的中國音樂。

☐ There's going to be a free concert at the park this weekend if you're interested.

如果您感興趣的話，這個週末在公園有一場免費的音樂會。

☐ I know a jazz club that serves food and drinks. The house band is pretty good.

我知道一家供應食物和飲料的爵士樂酒吧。他們店內的樂團非常棒。

☐ There are a couple of[2] places we can go to see some underground music.[3]

有好幾個地方我們可以去聽地下音樂。

☐ There is a $300 cover charge.[4] It includes a free drink.

這裡的服務費是三百元，含一杯免費飲料。

Word List

[1] symphony [ˋsɪmfənɪ] n. 交響樂
[2] a couple of 一些
[3] underground music 地下音樂

[4] cover charge [ˋkʌvə ͵tʃɑrdʒ] n. 服務費

90 去 KTV：出發和基本認識 🎵 MP3 91

KTV : Going and Basics

☐ I've made KTV reservations[1] for nine o'clock at the Cash Box in Xīméndīng.

我已經在西門町的錢櫃 KTV 訂了九點的包廂。

☐ KTV and karaoke are a little different. You'll like KTV.

KTV 和 karaoke 不太一樣。您會喜歡 KTV 的。

☐ KTV has private rooms with couches where people take turns[2] singing.

KTV 有私人包廂，裡面有沙發，人們可以輪流唱歌。

☐ Karaoke is where you sing in front of everyone in the bar.

Karaoke 是在酒吧中的眾人面前唱歌。

☐ If you don't want to sing, you don't have to. You can just kick back[3] and eat.

您如果不想唱歌，可以不要唱。您可以放輕鬆和吃東西。

☐ Don't worry. There are lots of English songs that you can choose to sing. It'll be fun!

放心。有許多英文歌曲可供您選唱。會很好玩的！

---

1 reservation [ˌrɛzəˋveʃən] n. 預訂
2 take turns 輪流
3 kick back【俚語】放鬆

Word List

Part 6　觀光、活動、娛樂　🚗　119

☐ Pick a song from the menu[1] and enter the number here.

從選單中挑選一首歌，然後在這裡輸入號碼。

☐ Choose a song and sing it however you want. Make it your own.

選一首歌，想怎麼唱都可以。把它變成您自己的歌。

☐ We can adjust[2] the pitch[3] and tempo[4] of the song to make it easier to sing.

我們可以調整歌曲的音調和節拍，讓這首歌好唱一點。

☐ Do you want to sing a duet[5] with me? How about this song?

您想不想和我合唱？唱這首如何？

☐ Hey, you've got a good voice. That sounded nice.

嘿，您有副好嗓子。真好聽。

☐ Let me teach you how to sing this Chinese song. It's easy.

我來教您唱這首中文歌曲。很簡單的。

Word List

1 menu [ˈmɛnju] n. 選單；菜單
2 adjust [əˈdʒʌst] v. 調整
3 pitch [pɪtʃ] n. 音高

4 tempo [ˈtɛmpo] n. 拍子；速度
5 duet [duˈɛt] n. 二重唱；二重奏

92 去 KTV：點心和離去

KTV : Snacks and Leaving

☐ Let me know if you'd like anything to eat or drink.

如果您想吃點什麼或喝點什麼，請告訴我。

☐ We're going to order a bunch of snacks and split them.

我們要叫一些零食點心一起吃。

☐ Take a look at the menu. I'll help you order anything you'd like.

您看一下菜單。您想叫什麼我會幫您點。

☐ If we need anything, just hit[1] the button on the wall.

如果我們需要什麼，只要按牆上這個按鈕就行了。

☐ There is a concession[2] area downstairs. We can go down there and get some drinks.

地下室有販賣區。我們可以下去買些飲料。

☐ The bill[3] is NT$3,200. Split seven ways, everyone needs to pay NT$457.

一共是新台幣三千兩百元。七人拆帳，一個人要付四百五十七元。

Word
List

1 hit [hɪt]【口語】按
2 concession [kən`sɛʃən] n.（公共娛樂場所等的）販賣區

3 bill [bɪl] n. 帳單

93 地點介紹：當代性
Introducing a Place : Contemporary

把一些訊息告訴你的訪客，讓對方留下印象並且為這個地方打廣告。

☐ The population[1] here is about the same as Canada—twenty-three million.

這裡的人口和加拿大差不多——二千三百萬人。

☐ Taiwan has over 8,000 convenience stores[2]—that's the world's highest store-to-person ratio.[3]

台灣大約有八千家便利商店——以商店和人口比例而言，居世界之冠。

☐ Our news media is like paparazzi[4]—they don't let anything get by[5] them.

我們的新聞媒體就像狗仔隊——他們絕不錯過任何線索。

☐ Trends[6] and gossip[7] spread and mutate[8] very quickly here.

這裡的流行和八卦傳播變質的速度非常快速。

☐ People here speak Mandarin and Shanghainese.

這裡的人說國語和上海話。

☐ The richest man in Taiwan is worth around US$5.4 billion—or so they say.

台灣第一富豪的身價大約是美金五十四億——聽說是如此。

Word List

1 population [ˌpɑpjəˈleʃən] n. 人口
2 convenience store [kənˈvinjəns ˌstor] n. 便利商店
3 ratio [ˈreʃo] n. 比率
4 paparazzi [ˌpɑpəˈrɑtsɪ] n. 狗仔隊（為 paparazzo 的複數）
5 get by 通過；躲過
6 trend [trɛnd] n. 趨勢；時尚
7 gossip [ˈgɑsəp] n. 八卦；閒話
8 mutate [ˈmjutet] v. 突變；變化

94 健行

Hiking

注意觀察訪客的健康狀況。如果對方的身體不錯，而你又遠遠超前，此時開個玩笑說：「Mr. Braddock, you're lagging behind.」（「布萊達克先生，你落後了。」），這是恰當的。否則，請參考下面的說法：

☐ The stairs are pretty steep/[1] slippery,[2] so be careful.

階梯很陡／滑，要小心。

☐ How are you doing? Want to take a rest?[3]

你還好嗎？要不要休息一下？

☐ Let's take a break[4] at this pavilion.[5] We should drink some water.

我們在這個涼亭休息一下。我們應該喝些水。

☐ Look at that huge spider web[6] over there.

您瞧那邊那個巨大的蜘蛛網。

☐ Go left/right at the next fork.[7]

下一條岔路時往左／右。

☐ Let me get a picture of you in front of that sign.

我幫您在這個指示牌前照張相。

Word List

1 steep [stip] adj. 陡峭的
2 slippery [ˋslɪpərɪ] adj. 滑的
3 take a rest 休息
4 take a break 休息

5 pavilion [pəˋvɪljən] n. 涼亭
6 spider web [ˋspaɪdə‚wɛb] n. 蜘蛛網
7 fork [fɔrk] n. 岔路；岔口

95 舞廳和「其他」夜店
Dance Clubs and "Other" Clubs

x
併非所有的訪客都喜歡夜生活，但是老一輩的人可能還是會對這項提議感興趣。您必須事先做好功課，安排好計畫。

☐ Do you want to go dancing? I know a place with a good DJ tonight.

您想去跳舞嗎？我知道一個地方，今天晚上的 DJ 很棒。

☐ See that guy over there? He's a pretty famous TV celebrity.[1]

您看到那邊那個人嗎？他是個蠻知名的電視名人。

☐ The bathroom is that way. Can I get you a drink while you're away?

洗手間在那邊。您離開的時候要不要我幫您拿杯酒？

☐ Let's go dance for a while. We can work off[2] some stress.

咱們去跳個舞吧，這樣可以釋放一些壓力。

☐ Let's go outside for a breath of fresh air. It's a little stuffy[3] in here.

我們出去外面透透氣，裡面有一點悶。

☐ My boss wants to take you to an escort[4] bar. Are you comfortable with that?

我的主管要帶您去有小姐作陪的酒吧。您習慣那種場合嗎？

Word List

1 celebrity [səˋlɛbrətɪ] n. 名人；名流
2 work off 發洩；排除
3 stuffy [ˋstʌfɪ] adj. 通風不良的

4 escort [ˋɛskɔrt] n. 隨侍者；陪伴者；護送者

124 迎賓 *900* 句典

Part 7
購物
Shopping

☐ What are you looking for? Something formal[1] or something casual?[2]

您在找什麼樣的衣服？正式的還是休閒的？

☐ How much do you want to spend? What's your price range?[3]

您打算花多少錢？您的預算範圍是多少？

☐ I'll take you to an area with lots of shops and we can browse around.

我會帶您去一個有許多商店的地方，這樣我們就可以到處逛逛。

☐ I'll ask if they have more of this color in the back.

我去問他們裡面還有沒有這種顏色的。

☐ They said they can order it for you. Can you come back tomorrow to pick it up?

他們說可以幫您訂。您明天可以回來拿嗎？

☐ Would you like to try that one? The dressing room[4] is over there.

您要不要試穿那一件？試衣間在那邊。

Word List

1 formal [ˋfɔrml] adj. 正式的
2 casual [ˋkæʒuəl] adj. 非正式的；不拘禮節的
3 price range [ˋpraɪs ˏrendʒ] n. 價錢範圍；預算範圍
4 dressing room 試衣間；更衣室

97 衣服：合身和顏色

Clothes : Fit[1] and Color

☐ How does it fit? Do you need a larger or smaller size?

合身嗎？您需要大一點還是小一點的尺寸？

☐ This is the biggest/smallest size they have.

這是他們最大／小的尺寸。

☐ They'll shorten[2] the pants free of charge.[3]

他們會免費把長褲改短一些。

☐ Do you like the color? I think it looks nice.

您喜歡這個顏色嗎？我覺得很好看。

☐ It looks nice on you.

您穿起來挺適合的。

☐ Hmm. Maybe you should try this one.

嗯……或許您應該試試這一件。

---

1 fit [fɪt] v.（衣服）合身；適合
2 shorten [ˈʃɔrtn̩] v. 使縮短；使減少
3 free of charge 免費

98 必需品：個人衛生用品

Necessities[1] : Personal Care

如果你的訪客需要幫忙找個人必備用品，可試試下列用語。

☐ You need some "lens[2] solution?"[3] Can you tell me what that is for?

您需要「隱形眼鏡清潔藥水」？您可不可以告訴我那是做什麼用的？

☐ "Lip balm?"[4] What does it look like? Can you describe it for me?

「護脣膏」？長什麼樣子？可以請您為我形容一下嗎？

☐ Watsons should have what you need. It has a big green sign.

屈臣氏應該有您需要的東西。那家店有大型的綠色招牌。

☐ We should be able to find that at a department store.

這東西我們在百貨公司應該可以找得到。

☐ I think we can find what you're looking for at the supermarket downstairs.

我想您在找的東西我們在樓下的超市可以買得到。

☐ I have a friend who can help us find that. Let me call him/her.

我有個朋友可以幫我們找那個東西。我來打電話給他／她。

Word List

1 necessity [nə`sɛsətɪ] n. 必需品
2 lens [lɛnz] n. 鏡片
3 solution [sə`luʃən] n. 溶劑；溶液

4 lip balm [`lɪp‚bɑm] 護脣膏

99 必需品：其他雜物

Necessities : Odds and Ends

如果你的訪客在找電池之類或其他維修物件，請使用下列用語。

☐ You need some glue to fix your suitcase? Let's try a hardware[1] store.

您需要接著劑來修理您的行李箱？咱們到五金店去找找。

☐ Your glasses are broken? No problem. There's an optometrist[2] nearby.

您的眼鏡破了？沒問題，附近有家眼鏡行。

☐ We can get batteries at a convenience store. What size do you need?

我們可以在便利商店買到電池。您需要幾號的？

☐ If you need packing tape,[3] let's check a stationery[4] store.

如果您需要打包用的膠帶，咱們可以到文具店去看看。

☐ Looks like you need a cheap suitcase to get your souvenirs home. I know a place.

看來您需要一個便宜的行李箱把紀念品帶回去。我知道有個地方。

☐ Need a USB cable for your computer? I've got one I can lend you.

您的電腦需要 USB 接線嗎？我有一條可以借給您。

Word
List

1 hardware [`hɑrd.wɛr] n. 金屬器件；五金器具
2 optometrist [ɑp`tɑmətrɪst] n. 驗光師；配鏡師

3 packing tape [`pækɪŋ .tep] n. 打包用膠帶
4 stationery [`steʃən.ɛrɪ] n. 文具

100 電子產品
Electronics[1]

☐ What exactly are you looking for? Can you show me a picture?

您究竟在找什麼？能不能拿張圖片讓我看看嗎？

☐ The electronics market has lots of private vendors. Let's browse around a bit first.

電子產品商場有許多私人店舖。咱們先逛一圈。

☐ The price includes the hard drive[2], the case, and formatting[3] the disk.

這價格包含硬碟機、外殼，和磁碟格式化。

☐ This one has a lifetime[4] warranty. [5]

這個產品有終生保固。

☐ All of the cables[6] and accessories[7] are over here.

全部的電線和配件都在這邊。

☐ Memory cards[8] are all on the second floor.

記憶卡都在二樓。

Word List

1 electronics [ɪlɛk`trɑnɪks] n. 電子學
2 hard drive [`hɑrd `draɪv] n. 硬碟機
3 format [`fɔrmæt] v. 為……編排格式；格式化
4 lifetime [`laɪf.taɪm] adj. 終身的
5 warranty [`wɔrəntɪ] n. 保證書
6 cable [`kebl] n. 電纜
7 accessory [æk`sɛsərɪ] n. 配件；附件
8 memory card [`mɛmərɪ.kɑrd] n. 記憶卡

101 書籍
Books

☐ What kind of book are you looking for?
您在找哪一類的書？

☐ You can write the name down and I'll help you find it.
您可以把書名寫下來，我來幫您找。

☐ Let's ask the clerk[1] to see if they have that book.
我們去問店員看他們有沒有那本書。

☐ The clerk says to look in the (non) fiction[2] section.
店員說去（非）小說區找找看。

☐ It may be easier to order it online.
線上訂購或許會比較方便。

☐ If you need a good Chinese-English dictionary, this white one is good.
如果您需要一本漢英字典，這一本白色的不錯。

Word
List

1 clerk [klɜk] n. 店員；辦事員
2 (non) fiction [(nɑn) `fɪkʃən] n. （非）小說

☐ Beijing Roast Duck is a Chinese specialty.[1] You can't visit without trying some.

北京烤鴨是一道中國的名菜。你來此拜訪絕不可不嚐嚐。

☐ Vacuum-packed[2] Beijing Duck will keep for several weeks.

真空包裝的北京烤鴨可以保存好幾週。

☐ When we're in Shanghai, I'll take you to get a cheongsam.[3] You can get one tailor-made.[4]

我們到上海的時後，我會帶妳去買旗袍。妳可以訂作一件。

☐ I have an American friend who's crazy about[5] pineapple cakes.

我有個美國朋友愛死鳳梨酥了。

☐ A bottle of rice wine would make a nice souvenir.

一瓶米酒是不錯的紀念品。

☐ I'm sure you could get that cheaper at the duty-free shop at the airport.

我相信您可以在機場免稅商店用更低的價錢買到那個。

Word List

1 specialty [ˋspɛʃəltɪ] n. 特產；名產
2 vacuum-packed [ˋvækjuəmˏpækt] adj. 真空包裝的
3 cheongsam [tʃɛˋɔŋsɑm] n. 中國旗袍
4 tailor-made [ˋteləˋmed] adj. 量身訂作的
5 be crazy about 醉心於；熱中於

103 紀念品：小東西
Souvenirs : Small Items

☐ We should take the train to Suzhou to do some souvenir shopping.

我們應該搭火車到蘇州去買些紀念品。

☐ If you want a personalized gift, how about getting a name chop?[1]

如果您希望禮物具有個人風格，弄顆印章如何？

☐ There's a handicraft[2] store near here. I bet[3] you could find something you would like.

這附近有家手工藝品店。我確信您一定可以找到您想要的東西。

☐ This area is famous for its decorative rocks.

這個地區以裝飾用的石頭出名。

☐ A lot of people buy these little good-luck charms[4] when they visit the temple.

許多人在參觀這座廟的時候會買這些小幸運符。

☐ If your friends aren't that picky,[5] you should be able to find something at the airport gift shop.

如果您的朋友不是很挑剔的話，您在機場的禮品店應該就可以買到東西。

Word List

1 name chop [`nem, tʃɑp] n. 私章；印章
2 handicraft [`hændɪ, kræft] n. 手工藝
3 bet [bɛt] v. 敢斷定；確信

4 charm [tʃɑrm] n. 護身符；符咒
5 picky [`pɪkɪ] adj. 挑剔的

104 銷售與殺價
Sales and Bargaining

 MP3 105

使用下列句子幫助你的訪客爭取好價錢。

☐ The items here are all twenty percent off. Those are two for one.

這裡這些東西全部打八折；那些則是買二送一。

☐ This big "8" means 80% of the original[1] price, not 80% off.

這個大大的數字 8 的意思是按照原價打八折，並不是打二折。

☐ If you spend more than four hundred, he'll take fifteen percent off.

如果您消費超過四百元，他會打八五折。

☐ That's too much for that. I'll offer half and see what she says.

那東西那樣太貴了。我會出半價，然後看她怎麼說。

☐ She says she can't go lower than two hundred. Let's just walk away.

她說不能低於兩百元。那我們走吧。

☐ He says he'll sell it for one fifty (150). What's your bottom line? [2]

他說要賣一百五十元。你的底線是多少？

Word List

■ original [ə`rɪdʒən] adj. 原本的
■ bottom line [`bɑtəm`laɪn]
　 n. 底線；最後結果

 迎賓 900 句典

105 付款
Payment

☐ It may be a little cheaper if you pay cash.

如果付現會便宜一點。

☐ Do you have any smaller bills?

您有小鈔嗎？

☐ I don't know if they take credit cards. Let me ask.

我不知道他們是否接受刷卡。我來問問看。

☐ You can give her the money. She'll take it to the cashier[1] and bring you the change.[2]

您可以把錢給她。她會拿給收銀員，然後把找回的零錢拿給您。

☐ She's asking if you'd like them to put the company number on the receipt.[3]

她在問您是否需要在收據打上公司的統編。

☐ You can apply[4] to have your tax[5] refunded[6] when you leave the country.

您離開本國時可以申請退稅。

Word List

1 cashier [kæ`ʃɪr] n. 出納員；收銀員
2 change [tʃendʒ] n. 零錢；找回的零錢
3 receipt [rɪ`sit] n. 收據
4 apply [ə`plaɪ] v. 申請
5 tax [tæks] n. 稅
6 refund [rɪ`fʌnd] n. 退還；退款

Part8

任務開始

Doing Work

106 訪客的行程：每日的
Your Guest's Schedule : Daily

☐ What time will you be ready to meet tomorrow? Is 10:00 too early?

您明天早上什麼時候可以碰面？十點會不會太早？

☐ If you'd like me to come a little later, that's no problem.

如果您希望我晚一點來，沒問題。

☐ I'll meet you in the lobby[1] at 10:30 then.

我十點半在大廳和您碰面。

☐ Your presentation is scheduled[2] for 2:00.

您做簡報的時間安排在兩點。

☐ Our flight to Kaohsiung leaves at 5:30, so we'll have to leave the office by 4:00.

我們到高雄的班機在五點半起飛，所以我們四點就必須離開辦公室。

☐ We'll have dinner with the technology people at 6:30 or 7:00.

我們六點半或七點和技術部門的人晚餐有約。

Word List

[1] lobby [ˈlɑbɪ] n. （飯店、旅館等的）大廳
[2] schedule [ˈskɛdʒʊl] v. 排定；把……安排在

107 訪客的行程：每週的
Your Guest's Schedule : Weekly

☐ We'd like you to give a short talk to the IT department[1] on Monday.

我們希望您星期一能到資訊科技部門做個簡短的演講。

☐ Our flight departs at 9:30 Tuesday morning.

我們的班機在星期二早上九點半出發。

☐ They're expecting us at the factory sometime Wednesday afternoon.

他們星期三下午會在工廠等候我們。

☐ We don't have anything scheduled for Thursday, so we can squeeze[2] in some sightseeing if you'd like.

我們星期四沒有安排任何行程，所以如果您要的話，我們可以把觀光的行程擠進去。

☐ The CEO[3] would like to invite you to dinner Friday evening.

總裁想邀請您星期五晚上一起吃晚餐。

☐ I'd be happy to show you around town on Saturday before your flight.

星期六在您搭飛機之前，我很樂意帶您到市區逛逛。

Part 8 任務開始

Word List

1 IT department 資訊科技部門
(IT = Information Technology
[ˌɪnfəˈmeʃən tɛkˈnɑlədʒɪ])

2 squeeze [skwiz] v. 擠；壓
3 CEO 總裁 (= chief executive officer
[ˈtʃif ɪgˈzɛkjutɪv ˈɔfɪsɚ])

108 公司簡介
Company Overview

MP3 109

☐ Yoyodyne was established[1] in 1961 by Cornelius Chang.

友友戴恩成立於 1961 年，創辦人是克納里斯・張。

☐ Originally, the company made transistors[2] and other small electronics.

最初，本公司製造的是電晶體和其他小型電子產品。

☐ In the 70s we diversified[3] into chemicals and heavy machinery.[4]

在 1970 年期間，我們往多元化方面發展，生產化學產品和重機械。

☐ We opened our first overseas manufacturing[5] plant[6] in 1981.

我們在 1981 年成立第一家海外製造廠。

☐ We acquired[7] Dynamix in 1997 and opened our London office in 2006.

我們在 1997 年取得迪納米克斯，並於 2006 年在倫敦成立分公司。

☐ Today we're one of the largest producers of computer peripherals[8] in the world.

今日我們是全世界電腦週邊設備產品最大的製造廠商之一。

Word List

1 establish [əˋstæblɪʃ] v. 建立；創立
2 transistor [trænˋzɪstə] n. 電晶體
3 diversify [daɪˋvɝsə͵faɪ] v. 使多樣化（如增加產品種類）
4 machinery [məˋʃinərɪ] n.【集合詞】機械；機器

5 manufacturing [͵mænjəˋfæktʃərɪŋ] adj. 製造（業）的
6 plant [plænt] n. 工廠
7 acquire [əˋkwaɪr] v. 獲得
8 peripheral [pəˋrɪfərəl] n. 電腦的週邊設備

109 學校和機構概況
Campus and Organization Overview

學校 ☐ Our school was set up in 1948 and has a sister campus in China.

我們學校成立於 1948 年，而且在中國有個姊妹校。

☐ The student body[1] is 65% undergraduates,[2] 30% graduate students[3], and 5% international students.

學生成員百分之六十五是大學生，百分之三十是研究生，百分之五是國際學生。

☐ We are currently revamping[4] several programs[5] to attract more foreign students and scholars.

我們目前正在修訂幾項課程以吸引更多外籍學生和學者。

公司 ☐ This (non-profit)[6] organization was founded[7] in 1986 with a grant[8] from the government.

本（非營利的）機構，獲得了政府的補助成立於 1986 年。

☐ We have a permanent[9] staff[10] of twenty and over fifty volunteer[11] workers.

我們有二十名正職員工和五十名以上的志工。

☐ Your visit is a great way for us to spread the word[12] on what we do.

您的來訪是我們宣傳我們所做的工作一個非常棒的方法。

Part 8 任務開始

Word List

■1 body [ˋbadɪ] n. 主體；主要部分
■2 undergraduate [ˌʌndɚˋgrædʒuɪt] n. 大學生
■3 graduate student [ˋgrædʒʊˌet ˋstjudn̩t] n. 研究生
■4 revamp [riˋvæmp] v. 換新；修改；改造
■5 program [ˋprogræm] n. 節目；計劃；課程；綱領；程式

■6 non-profit [nɑnˋprɑfɪt] adj. 非營利的
■7 found [faʊnd] v. 創立；建立
■8 grant [grænt] n. 承認；補助
■9 permanent [ˋpɝmənənt] adj. 永久的
■10 staff [stæf] n. 全體職員；員工
■11 volunteer [ˌvɑlənˋtɪr] adj. 自願的
■12 spread the word 散播消息

110 設施導覽
Facility Tour

MP3 111

☐ You're going to need to wear a hard hat[1] and safety goggles.[2] Put these on.

您必須戴上安全帽和護目鏡。請戴上吧。

☐ This facility was built five years ago and contains state-of-the-art[3] equipment.

這套設施是五年前建造的,它擁有最先進的裝置。

☐ Most of the equipment you see was imported[4] from Germany.

您眼前看到的大部分設備都是從德國進口的。

☐ That's about all there is to see here. Let's move on to the next area.

這裡能看的差不多都看完了。我們移到下一區吧。

☐ This is where we package[5] the product.

這裡是我們的產品包裝區。

☐ We can produce over 3,000 units[6] a day when we're fully staffed.[7]

如果人員備齊,我們每天可以製造超過三千個。

Word List

1 hard hat [`hɑrd ˏhæt] n. 工地;安全帽
2 goggles [`gɑglz] n. 【複數型】護目鏡
3 state-of-the-art [`stet əv ðɪ `ɑrt] adj. 最先進的

4 import [ɪm`port] v. 進口
5 package [`pækɪdʒ] v. 包裝
6 unit [`junɪt] n. 單位;部門;組件
7 staff [stæf] v. 給……配備職員

111 設施和校園導覽
Facility and Campus Tour

設施 ☐ Currently we have over two hundred fifty people working here.
目前我們有超過兩百五十個員工在這裡工作。

☐ There is a cafeteria on-site.[1] We'll be going there for refreshments.[2]
場區就有自助餐廳。我們將會到那裡去用點心。

☐ This concludes[3] our tour. We hope you have enjoyed it.
我們的參觀到這裡結束，希望您喜歡。

校園 ☐ Welcome to our university. We hope you enjoy your stay.[4]
歡迎來到我們的大學。希望您停留的這段時間玩得愉快。

☐ This building is one of the oldest on campus. It houses[5] the department of history.
這棟建築是學園中最古老的建築，裡面是歷史系。

☐ Next we'll visit the library, student center[6], and then the dormitory[7]complex.[8]
我們接著要參觀圖書館、學生活動中心，然後是宿舍綜合設施。

Word List

[1] on-site [`ɑn,saɪt] adj. 在原場所的
[2] refreshments [rɪ`frɛʃmənts] n. 【複數型】茶點
[3] conclude [kən`klud] v. 結束
[4] stay [ste] n. 停留；逗留
[5] house [haʊs] v. 包含；收藏
[6] student center 學生活動中心
[7] dormitory [`dɔrmə,torɪ] n. 宿舍
[8] complex [`kɑmplɛks] n. 綜合設施

112 簡報：準備
Presentations : Preparations

☐ This room has a laptop[1] with Internet access,[2] a projector, and a white board.

這個房間有一台可上網的筆記型電腦、一個投影機和一面白板。

☐ Will you need any special equipment or assistance[3] with your presentation?

您做簡報時需要其他的設備或協助嗎？

☐ Could you make a list of the stuff you'll need?

您可不可以將需要的東西列出清單？

☐ I've made copies of your handouts.[4] Is there anything else I can help you with?

我已經將您的講義影印好了。還需要我幫什麼忙嗎？

☐ Could you give me a short biography[5]? I'm going to say a few words to introduce you.

您可不可以給我一份簡短的自傳？我將講幾句話介紹您。

☐ You'll go on right after Mr. Yang, the CTO.[6]

您將緊接著在技術總監楊先生後面報告。

Word List

1 laptop [`læp͵tɑp] n. 膝上型電腦
2 access [`æksɛs] n. 接近；取得
3 assistance [ə`sɪstəns] n. 協助
4 handout [`hænd͵aʊt] n. 講義；傳單
5 biography [baɪ`ɑgrəfɪ] n. 傳記
6 CTO 技術總監（= Chief Technical Officer [`tʃif `tɛknɪkl̩ `ɔfɪsə]）

113 簡報：現場
Presentations : On the Scene[1]

MP3 114

介紹 ☐ I'd like to thank Mr. Smith for coming all the way[2] from Dublin[3] to be here with us today.

今天我要感謝史密斯先生大老遠從都柏林來到我們這裡。

☐ It's truly an honor to have Mr. Smith join us here this morning.

今天早上很榮幸地能邀請史密斯先生來和我們在一起。

☐ Let's all give Mr. Smith a warm Yoyodyne welcome.

請大家給史密斯先生來一個友友戴恩式的熱烈歡迎。

技術
問題 ☐ Looks like we're having a technical problem. Bear with[4] us.

看來我們碰到了一個技術上的問題。請耐心等一會兒。

☐ Why don't we take a ten-minute break for refreshments?

我們何不休息十分鐘用些點心？

☐ I'm so sorry about that, Mr. Smith. I think we can start again in a few minutes.

史密斯先生，真是對不起。我想我們過幾分鐘就可以重新開始。

Word
List

1 on the scene 現場；當場
2 all the way 一路；大老遠
3 Dublin [ˋdʌblɪŋ] n. 都柏林（愛爾蘭的首都）

4 bear with 忍耐

Part 8 任務開始 145

Part
8
任務開始

114 和本地人士見面
Meeting local people

MP3 115

☐ Please let me know if there's anyone you'd like to meet.

如果您想見哪個人，就請告訴我。

☐ I've arranged for you to meet Mr. Leung, a very influential[1] scholar[2] here.

我已經安排您和梁先生見面，他是我們這裡一位非常有影響力的學者。

☐ There's a workshop[3] at the Academia Sinica[4] tomorrow. It'll be a good chance to network.[5]

明天在中研院有個研討會。這是個建立關係的好機會。

☐ The director of the finance department is really interested in meeting you.

財務部門的主管很想和您見面。

☐ We'll be able to talk with the marketing people over lunch on Wednesday.

我們將可以利用星期三午餐時和行銷部門的人聊聊。

☐ I'll introduce you to the people running[6] the Shanghai operation[7] at the conference.[8]

我會在會議上把您介紹給負責上海地區營運的人員認識。

Word List

1 influential [ˌɪnfluˈɛnʃəl] adj. 有影響力的
2 scholar [ˈskɑlə] n. 學者
3 workshop [ˈwɜkˌʃɑp] n. 研討會
4 Academia Sinica [ˌækəˈdimɪə ˈsɪnɪkə] n. 中央研究院

5 network [ˈnɛtˌwɜk] v. 與他人建立關係
6 run [rʌn] v. 經營；管理
7 operation [ˌɑpəˈreʃən] n. 操作；運作；經營；手術
8 conference [ˈkɑnfərəns] n. 會議；協商會

115 貿易展
Trade Show

☐ Let's check in at the counter.[1]
我們去櫃檯報到吧。

☐ We need to exchange our business cards[2] for entrance[3] passes.
我們必須用名片換取通行證。

☐ Most of the interesting booths[4] are in Building C.
比較有趣的攤位大多都在 C 棟大樓。

☐ Could you man[5] the booth for a while and answer questions?
您可不可以顧一下攤位,回答一下問題?

☐ Let's meet in front of the Yoyodyne booth at 3:00.
我們三點在友友戴恩的攤位前面碰面。

☐ There's going to be a lecture[6] about investment[7] at 4:30 if you're interested.
如果您有興趣的話,四點半有一場關於投資的演講。

Part 8 任務開始

Word List

1 counter [ˈkaʊntə] n. 櫃檯
2 business card 名片
3 entrance [ˈɛntrəns] n. 進入;入場
4 booth [buθ] n. 攤位;電話亭;警衛室;雅座

5 man [mæn] v. 配置人員;(把人)安排於職位、崗位
6 lecture [ˈlɛktʃə] n. 演講;授課
7 investment [ɪnˈvɛstmənt] n. 投資

☐ Late registration[2] is OK. You'll just have to pay NT$1,500 at the door.

晚報名沒有關係。您只要在門口繳交一千五百元即可。

☐ Amy, from my team, will be there to translate for you.

我這一組的愛咪會擔任您的翻譯。

☐ Will you have a chance to read over[3] the materials before the session?[4]

會前您會有機會仔細看過這份資料嗎？

☐ Which session are you most interested in attending?

您最想參加哪一場？

☐ Would you like to stay for the entire event, or do you want to sneak[5] out early?

您想待完整場活動，還是提早開溜？

☐ If it's boring we'll just take off.[6]

如果很無聊，我們就離開。

Word List

1 seminar [ˋsɛməˏnɑr] n. 專題討論會
2 registration [ˏrɛdʒɪˋstreʃən] n. 登記；註冊
3 read over 精讀
4 session [ˋsɛʃən] n. 開會期間；活動期間；會議
5 sneak [snik] v. 偷偷地進、出
6 take off 離開

117 研討會和會議：在活動現場
Seminars and Conferences : At the Event

☐ Have you been to one of these before?

您以前參加過類似的活動嗎？

☐ Could I take a look at your program?

我可以看一下您的預訂表嗎？

☐ What did you think of the first guy's presentation?

您覺得第一個報告的人表現如何？

☐ The moderator[1] needs to do a better job of controlling the time.

會議主持人應該要把時間控制好。

☐ The discussants[2] on this panel[3] were more interesting than the speaker.

這個小組的討論者比演講者有趣多了。

☐ I think we can leave after the first afternoon session.

我想我們下午第一場會之後就可以離開了。

Part
8

任務開始

Word List

1 moderator [ˈmɑdəˌretə] n. 會議主席；主持人

2 discussant [dɪˈskʌsənt] n. 參加討論的人

3 panel [ˈpænl] n. 專題討論小組

☐ So, what's the next step?

那麼，下一步是什麼？

☐ I'd like to set up[1] another meeting to discuss where we go from here.[2]

我想安排另外一場會議討論我們接下來怎麼做。

☐ Let's just take it step-by-step[3] and see what happens.

我們一步一步來，看看後續如何發展。

☐ Let us run the numbers first, and we'll take it from there.[4]

我們先檢視一下數字，然後我們再從那兒著手。

☐ It looks really good on paper, so I'm sure we'll consider it carefully.

書面上看起來很不錯，所以我想我們一定會仔細考慮。

☐ I think we need a little time to evaluate[5] your proposal, but we're obviously[6] very interested.

我想我們需要一點時間評估你們的提案，但我們顯然對這項提案非常感興趣。

Word List

1 set up 設立；安排
2 where we go from here 我們接下來怎麼做
3 step-by-step 一步一步

4 We'll take it from there. 我們再從那兒著手。
5 evaluate [ɪˋvæljʊˌet] v. 對……評估
6 obviously [ˋɑbvɪəslɪ] adv. 明顯地

119 未來的合作：態度樂觀
Future Cooperation : Optimistic[1]

MP3 120

☐ I'm really optimistic about the project.
我對這項企劃案非常樂觀。

☐ It seems like a win-win[2] situation for everyone.
這對大家都是雙贏的局面。

☐ I'm pretty confident[3] that this is going to happen.
我非常有信心，這個案子一定會成功。

☐ I'm really looking forward to working with you on this.
我非常期待能和您合作進行這個案子。

☐ It looks like we'll probably be seeing a lot more of each other.
看樣子我們可能會常常見面了。

☐ It looks like it's going to be a very successful trip.
看來這是趟非常成功的行程。

Part 8 任務開始

Word List
1 optimistic [ˌɑptəˋmɪstɪk] adj. 樂觀的
2 win-win 雙贏
3 confident [ˋkɑnfədənt] adj. 確信的；有自信的

Part 9

解決問題

Problem Solving

☐ You look a little tired. Are you feeling OK?

您看起來好像有點累。您還好吧？

☐ Are you sure it's just jet lag?[2]

您確定這只是時差的關係嗎？

☐ It sounds like your cold is getting worse. How are you feeling?

您的感冒聽起來變嚴重了。您現在覺得怎麼樣？

☐ Is your stomach bothering you?

您的胃不舒服嗎？

☐ Do you have a fever?[3]

您發燒了嗎？

☐ How's your knee feeling today? Is it any better than yesterday?

您今天覺得膝蓋怎麼樣？是否比昨天好一些？

Word List

1 injury [ˈɪndʒərɪ] n. 受傷

2 jet lag [ˈdʒɛt͵læg] n. （因搭噴射機長程旅行而產生之）時差

3 fever [ˈfivə] n. 發燒

121 生病和受傷：提供建議

Illness and Injury : Making Suggestions

☐ Do you have something to take for it?

您有藥吃嗎？

☐ I could run down to the drug store[1] and get you some medicine.

我可以到藥局跑一趟幫您買一些藥。

☐ It sounds serious. Maybe we should postpone[2] your presentation.

聽起來嚴重。或許我們應該將您簡報的時間延後。

☐ Why don't you just take the day off[3] and rest? We can reschedule.

您為什麼不請一天假休息？我們可以重新安排時程。

☐ Let's go to the hospital to have it looked at.

我們去醫院檢查一下。

☐ Everything is going to be OK. I'm calling an ambulance[4] now.

不會有什麼事的。我現在就打電話叫救護車。

Word List

[1] drug store [`drʌg ˌstor] n. 藥房
[2] postpone [post`pon] v. 使延期
[3] take a day off 休假一天

[4] ambulance [`æmbjələns] n. 救護車

122 郵寄東西到國外
Mailing Things Abroad

MP3 123

☐ I can go with you to the post office.
我可以和您一起去郵局。

☐ Two-day service costs NT$1,400.
兩天送件的服務要一千四百元台幣。

☐ Surface mail[1] is the cheapest, but it'll take six to eight weeks to arrive.
普通郵件最便宜，但是通常要六至八週才會送到。

☐ Write the recipient's[2] address here. Your hotel address goes here.
收件人的地址寫在這裡，您的飯店地址寫在這裡。

☐ You need to check[3] this box, and itemize[4] the contents[5] here.
您必須在這個格子內打勾，然後在這裡詳列內容物。

☐ Seal[6] the box and stick[7] the label[8] here. OK, it's ready to go.
把箱子封好並在這裡貼上標籤。好了，一切就緒。

Word List

[1] surface mail [ˋsɝfɪs͵mel] n. 普通平信郵件；平信
[2] recipient [rɪˋsɪpɪənt] n. 收信人；接受者
[3] check [tʃɛk] v. 打勾
[4] itemize [ˋaɪtəm͵aɪz] v. 詳列；逐項列記
[5] content [ˋkɑntɛnt] n.（常用複數）內容
[6] seal [sil] v. 密封
[7] stick [stɪk] v. 黏貼
[8] label [ˋlebl̩] n. 標籤

123 通訊
Communications

MP3 124

要處理傳真、電子郵件、網路、手機、列印或影印時，可使用下列句子。

☐ You can send and receive faxes at convenience stores.

您可以在便利商店傳送和接收傳真。

☐ Lots of places have wireless Internet access now.

現在許多地方都可以無線上網。

☐ In a pinch,[1] you can always use an Internet café[2] to check your email.

在必要時，您可以利用網咖收發電子郵件。

☐ We can get you a temporary[3] cell phone account[4] at a convenience store.

我們可以在便利商店幫您弄一個臨時的手機門號。

☐ If you don't mind, I have an old cell phone I can lend you.

如果您不介意，我有個舊的手機可以借您。

☐ Our intern[5] can help you with any documents[6] you need to print or copy.

我們的實習生可以幫您處理須列印或影印的文件。

Word List

[1] in a pinch 在必要時；在危急時（pinch [pɪntʃ] n. 緊急情況）
[2] Internet café [ˋɪntɚnɛt kəˋfe] n. 網咖
[3] temporary [ˋtɛmpəˏrɛrɪ] adj. 臨時的；暫時的
[4] account [əˋkaʊnt] n. 帳戶；戶頭；門號
[5] intern [ɪnˋtɝn] n. 實習生
[6] document [ˋdɑrkjəmənt] n. 文件；證件

124 訪客的飯店出問題

Problems at Your Guest's Hotel

MP3 125

☐ Is everything all right with the room?

您的房間一切都沒問題吧？

☐ I'll sort it out[1] with the staff right away.

我會立刻找服務人員處理這個問題。

☐ They'll be sending someone this afternoon to fix it.

他們下午會派人來修理。

☐ Would you like to move to a different hotel or just another room?

您想換一家飯店還是換房間就好？

☐ I'll have someone come by[2] and take care of the bill for you.

我會請人過去幫您處理帳單。

☐ I'll come over right away.

我會立刻過來。

Word List

1 sort out 處理；解決
2 come by （順路）到

 158 迎賓 900 句典

125 衣服和洗衣間
Clothes and Laundry[1]

☐ There's a self-serve laundry room in the basement.[2]

地下室有個自助洗衣間。

☐ The hotel laundry service is too expensive. I can recommend[3] a place.

飯店的洗衣服務太貴了。我可以推薦您另外一個地方。

☐ Let me know if there are any special cleaning instructions.[4]

如果有任何特別指示的洗滌方式,請告訴我。

☐ It's NT$39 to wash and press[5] a shirt.

清洗和熨燙襯衫的費用是台幣三十九元。

☐ They can have it done tomorrow afternoon.

他們明天下午就可以處理好。

☐ You're going to be here for a while. I'll lend you my ironing board[6] and iron.[7]

您會在這裡待上一陣子。我會把我的燙衣板和熨斗借給您。

Word List

1 laundry [`lɔndrɪ] n. 要洗的衣物;洗衣店;洗
衣間
2 basement [`besmənt] n. 地下室
3 recommend [ˌrɛkə`mɛnd] v. 推薦

4 instruction [ɪn`strʌkʃən] n. 操作說明
5 press [prɛs] v. 燙平(衣服)
6 ironing [`aɪənɪŋ] board n. 燙衣板
7 iron [`aɪən] n. 熨斗(可作動詞)

126 物品遺失或遭竊

Lost or Stolen Items

如果你的訪客告訴你東西不見了，下面是你可以回應的句子。

☐ Oh, no! That's terrible. Where did you last see it?

喔，不會吧！真是糟糕！您最後一次是什麼時候看到它的？

☐ Are you sure it's not back at the hotel?

您確定沒有留在飯店裡嗎？

☐ I'll call the MRT and see if someone turned it in.[1] It may be in the lost and found.[2]

我會打電話到捷運站，看是否有人撿到交出來。東西可能在失物招領處。

☐ Did you leave it in the cab?[3] Let me call the cab companies.

您是不是留在計程車裡了？我來打電話給計程車行。

☐ Did you see the person who stole it?

您是否有看到偷東西的人？

☐ We'll need to go to the local police station to file[4] a report.

我們必須去本地的警察局報案。

Word List

[1] turn in 交出；歸還
[2] lost and found 失物招領處
[3] cab [kæb] n. 計程車

[4] file [faɪl] v. 移……歸檔；提出（訴訟等）

127 電腦方面的問題
Computer Problems

☐ Let me see what I can do.

讓我看看我能做什麼。

☐ I'll have one of our IT guys take a look at it.

我會請一位我們的技術資訊人員來看看。

☐ I know a good repair shop.[1]

我知道有家維修店很不錯。

☐ What kind of computer is it? There's probably an official[2] repair shop in town.

是哪種類型的電腦？本地可能就有原廠牌的維修廠。

☐ I have one that you can borrow.

我有部電腦可以借您。

☐ It might be easier to buy a new one.

買一部新的或許會比較快。

Part
9

解
決
問
題

Word
List

[1] repair shop [rɪˋpɛr ˏʃɑp] n. 維修場
[2] official [əˋfɪʃəl] adj. 正式的；官方的

128 簽證的問題
Visa[1] Problems

☐ I'm afraid there's a problem with your paperwork.

您的書面文件恐怕有問題。

☐ You'll have to pay a fine[2] if you overstay[3] your visa.

您的簽證如果過期,會被罰款。

☐ Let me see if it's possible to extend[4] your visa.

我來看看能不能延長您的簽證。

☐ I'm sorry your visa application[5] wasn't approved.[6]

很遺憾,您的簽證申請沒有通過。

☐ You may have to leave the country and then come back.

您或許得先離開這個國家,然後再回來。

☐ It may be better to contact[7] your consulate[8] directly.

或許直接和您的領事館接洽會比較好。

Word List

1 visa [ˋvizə] n. 簽證
2 fine [faɪn] n. 罰款
3 overstay [͵ovəˋste] v. 逗留超過規定的時間
4 extend [ɪkˋstɛnd] v. 延長

5 application [͵æpləˋkeʃən] n. 申請;請求
6 approve [əˋpruv] adj. 認可;批准
7 contact [ˋkɑntækt] v. 與(人)連絡
8 consulate [ˋkɑnslɪt] n. 領事館

129 改變旅遊計畫
Change of Travel Plans

MP3 130

☐ I'm sorry that you have to leave on such short notice.[1]
我很遺憾您在接到通知後這麼短的時間內就必須離開。

☐ Would you like to extend your stay?
您想延長您停留的時間嗎？

☐ I'd be happy to make the arrangements.
我很樂意幫您安排一切。

☐ It shouldn't be hard to get a seat this time of year.
在一年中的這個時候要機位應該不會很難。

☐ Let me get in touch[2] with the airline and see what I can do.
我來聯絡一下航空公司，看看能做些什麼。

☐ I can recommend an excellent travel agency.[3] Let me get the number for you.
我可以推薦一家優質的旅行社。我來把號碼拿給您。

Part 9 解決問題

Word List

1 notice [ˋnotɪs] n. 通知（on short notice 指在接到通知後的短時間內）

2 get in touch（與……）聯繫；（與……）接觸

3 travel agency [ˋtrævl͵edʒənsɪ] n. 旅行社

Part 10

道別
Saying Farewell

130 結束參訪和未來的計畫

Accomplishments[1] of the Visit and Future Plans

☐ It was great working with you.

真高興能和您合作。

☐ Well, this has been a really productive[2] trip.

嗯，這趟旅程收穫非常豐富。

☐ I'm happy everything worked out[3] for us.

很高興我們一切都很順利成功。

☐ I think we can say your trip was a success.

我想我們可以說您這趟行程很成功。

☐ I'm really looking forward to working together on this.

我真的非常期待一起進行這個案子。

☐ I'll be in touch next week about what we discussed.

我下禮拜會與您連絡告訴您我們討論的結果。

Word List

1 accomplishment [əˋkɑmplɪʃmənt] n. 完成；實現
2 productive [prəˋdʌktɪv] adj. 有收穫的；富有成效的
3 work out 有好結果

131 行程總覽
Recapping[1] the Trip

☐ There were a few snags,[2] but basically everything went quite smoothly.

雖然有一些障礙，但是大致上一切進行得很順利。

☐ I'm glad the negotiations are behind us. Now we can get to work.

我很高興協商已經結束。我們現在可以開始著手工作了。

☐ Your presentation was really solid.[3] Everyone was very impressed.[4]

您的簡報內容非常紮實，大家都印象深刻。

☐ It was nice getting to know you a little better.

很高興能夠多了解您一些。

☐ It was fun having you. We'll have to do it again sometime.

能夠招待您真是開心。我們下次一定要再聚聚。

☐ When do you think you'll be back in this part of the world?

您想您什麼時候還會再回到世界的這一角（我們這個地方）？

Part
10
道別

Word List

1 recap [ˋriˏkæp] v. 重述要旨；摘要說明
2 snag [snæg] n. 障礙；阻礙
3 solid [ˋsɑlɪd] adj. 結實的；堅固的

4 impress [ɪmˋprɛs] v. 使銘記；使獲得深刻印象

132 道謝
Saying Thank You

☐ Thanks for making the trip all the way to Taiwan.

謝謝您大老遠來到台灣。

☐ I appreciate[1] all your help.

我要謝謝您的協助。

☐ We're grateful[2] for everything you've done for us.

我們非常感謝您為我們所做的一切。

☐ On behalf of[3] everyone at Yoyodyne, I'd like to thank you for your help with the workshop.[4]

我僅代表友友戴恩，謝謝您對研討會所做的協助。

☐ I know I speak for the entire department when I say "thank you."

我代表全體部門的人致謝。

☐ I truly appreciate your visit. It means a lot to all of us here.

我真心感謝您的到訪，這對我們意義非凡。

Word List

1 appreciate [əˋpriʃɪ͵et] v. 感激
2 grateful [ˋgretfəl] adj. 感激的
3 on behalf [bɪˋhæf] of 代表

4 workshop [ˋwɝk͵ʃɑp] n. 研討會

133 送禮
Gift Giving

□ We got you a little going-away present.

我們有一個小惜別禮物要送給您。

□ I got you a little something to remember us by.

我有一個會讓您想起我們的小東西要送給您。

□ I'd like to present you with a small gift as a token[1] of our appreciation.[2]

我想送您一個小禮物以表達我們的謝意。

□ I have some certificates[3] of appreciation to present to your group.

我有幾張感謝狀要送給你們的團隊。

□ Here's a little something from our department to say "thanks."

這是我們部門要送給您的一個小禮物，謝謝您。

□ Our director would like you to have this.

我們的主管希望您收下這個。

Word List

1 token [ˋtokən] n. 表徵；象徵；紀念品
2 appreciation [ə͵priʃɪˋeʃən] n. 感激；感謝
3 certificate [səˋtɪfəkɪt] n. 證明書

詢問 □ To be safe, could I have another one of your business cards?

為了安全起見，我可以跟您再要一張名片嗎？

□ Would you happen to[1] have Mr. Smith's email address?

您是否剛好有史密斯先生的電子郵件地址？

□ Could I trouble[2] you for Cynthia's contact[3] information?

我可以麻煩您告知辛希雅的聯絡方式嗎？

提議 □ Let me write down my telephone number and email address for you.

讓我寫下我的電話號碼和電子郵件地址給您。

□ I'll send you a text message[4] with Paul's number.

我會把保羅的電話號碼用簡訊傳給您。

□ I've printed up a list of contacts that you might find useful.

我已經列印了一張聯絡人名單，您可能會覺得有用。

---

1 happen to 發生
2 trouble [ˋtrʌbl] v.（表客氣時用）麻煩
3 contact [ˋkɑn͵tækt] n. 連絡；連絡人

4 text message [ˋtɛkst ͵mɛsɪdʒ] n. 簡訊

135 道再見
Saying Goodbye

□ It was great to finally meet you in person.[1]

真高興終於見到了您本人。

□ It's been a real pleasure getting to know you.

能夠認識您真是非常榮幸。

□ I hope you've enjoyed your stay as much as we have.

我希望您和我們一樣對於您的到訪感到非常愉快。

□ I've had a great time showing you around.

帶著您四處參觀，我非常開心。

□ Well, bon voyage.[2]

那，祝您一路順風。

□ OK. Take care. Until next time. Good-bye.

好了，多保重。下次再見了，拜拜。

Part
10

道
別

Word
List

1 in person 親自
2 bon voyage [ˌbɔnvɔɪˈɑʒ] 【法文】一路順風

 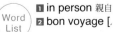

Part 11

後續

Following Up

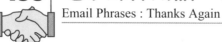

136 電子郵件用語：再度道謝
Email Phrases : Thanks Again

☐ I just wanted to thank you again for coming.

我只是想再度謝謝您的來訪。

☐ Thanks so much for allowing us to host you.

非常感謝您接受我們的招待。

☐ We appreciate all the help you gave us while you were here.

我們感謝您在這裡給予我們的一切協助。

☐ It was a real pleasure being able to show you around.

能夠帶您四處參觀是我的榮幸。

☐ On behalf of the whole department, I'd like to say, "Great presentation!"

僅代表全體部門，我想對您說：「您的簡報太精采了！」

☐ Your visit was a great success. Thank you.

您的到訪非常成功。謝謝您。

137 電子郵件用語：其他訊息

Email Phrases : Additional[1] Information

MP3 138

☐ I've attached[2] that spreadsheet[3] we talked about.

我附上了我們提過的試算表。

☐ I'll get those files to you in a day or two.

我過一兩天會把那些檔案傳給您。

☐ Those figures[4] I promised are on the way.[5]

我答應要提供給您的數字馬上就寄到。

☐ We'll have those product samples in the mail by the end of the week.

我們會將產品樣本在本週之前寄給您。

☐ I'll call you on Wednesday morning, your time, to confirm.[6]

我會在您那邊的星期三早上打電話給您，以做確認。

☐ I'd really appreciate that contact information, if you can send it at your earliest convenience.[7]

如果您方便，請儘早提供聯絡方式，我會非常感激。

Part II 後續

Word List

1 additional [ə`dɪʃən!] adj. 附加的；額外的
2 attach [ə`tætʃ] v. 使依附；使附屬
3 spreadsheet [`sprɛd,ʃit] n. 試算表
4 figure [`fɪgjə] n. 數字；金額

5 on the way 在途中
6 confirm [kə`fɜm] v. 確認；證實
7 at your earliest convenience
您方便時儘早

☐ I've attached some photos from your stay.

我附上了您參訪期間時拍的一些照片。

☐ The attached pictures were taken during the facility tour last Wednesday.

附上的照片是上星期三參觀工廠時拍的。

☐ Noah sent me the pictures he took at the banquet. See below.

諾亞把在晚宴上拍的照片寄給了我。請見下方。

☐ Wait until you see the pictures from the performance.[1] They came out[2] great.

等到您看到表演時拍的照片就知道。那些照片拍得真棒。

☐ I've reminded Jeff to send you the pictures from the trip.

我已經提醒傑夫把參訪時拍的照片寄給你。

☐ Be sure to email me the video you took.

記得把您拍的錄影帶用電子郵件寄給我。

Word List

1 performance [pɚˋfɔrməns] n. 演出；表演

2 come out （照片）洗出來

139 電子郵件用語：計畫下一次參訪 MP3 140

Email Phrases : Planning Another Visit

☐ When are we going to be able to get together again?

我們什麼時候可以再聚一聚？

☐ I really hope you'll be able to make another visit next spring.

我真的希望您明年春天可以再來訪。

☐ What's your schedule looking like in October for another visit?

依您十月的行程表看，能否安排下一次的參訪？

☐ Hopefully you can manage[1] another trip before the product launch[2] in February.

希望您能在二月產品推出之前設法再來一趟。

☐ It's looking like I won't be able to schedule the meeting in May as we had planned.

看來我沒辦法按我們事前計畫好的在五月排定那場會議了。

Part
II

後
續

Word
List

1 manage [ˋmænɪdʒ] v. 設法做到
2 launch [lɔntʃ] v. 推出；發行

140 電子郵件的樣本 I
Sample Email I

From : Sandy
To : Steve

Dear Steve,

I hope you had a smooth flight back. How's the jet lag? Be sure to send me those pictures from the night market.

See the attachment for the contact information I promised you.

Warm regards,
Sandy

寄件人：珊蒂
收件人：史蒂夫

史蒂夫您好：

希望您的回程一切順利。時差的問題還好吧？記得要把在夜市拍的那些照片寄給我。

我答應要給您的聯絡方式請見附檔。

珊蒂
謹啓

141 電子郵件的樣本 II

Sample Email II

From : Wen-Xiong Huang
To : Professor Cook

Dear Professor Cook,

It was a great pleasure to host you and your students. I trust you had an uneventful[1] flight back to Canada.

Please take a look at the two attachments. The first is an evaluation form that we'd like you to fill out and return to me via[2] email at your earliest convenience. The second is a picture of us taken at the farewell[3] banquet.

I'm looking forward to seeing you again next year.

Sincerely,
Wen-Xiong Huang, Ph.D.
Director of Academic Exchange

141

電子郵件的樣本 II
Sample Email II

寄件人：黃文雄
收件人：庫克教授

庫克教授您好：

能招待您和您的學生是我們莫大的榮幸。相信在您回加拿大的旅途上一路平安。

請見兩個附檔。第一個是評估表格，希望您填妥後，如果方便請儘快用電子郵件回覆給我。第二個是我們在送別晚宴上拍的照片。

期待明年再見到您。

學術交流主任

黃文雄教授
敬啟

Word List

1 uneventful [ˌʌnɪˋvɛntfəl] adj. 平靜無事的
2 via [ˋvaɪə] prep. 經由；憑藉
3 farewell [ˌfɛrˋwɛl] adj. 告別的

From : Christine
To : Samantha

Dear Samantha,

It was great to finally meet you in person. As we talked about during the facility tour, we should arrange for another meeting sometime in the fall to work out the details.

Like I promised, here is Roger's email address: rogerchen88@yoyodyne.com.tw. He knows you'll be writing and will be happy to assist.
Let me know if you have any questions.

Christine

電子郵件的樣本 III
Sample Email III

寄件人：克莉斯汀
收件人：莎曼珊

莎曼珊您好：

終於能夠見到您本人真是榮幸。正如我們參觀設施時所提到的，我們應該安排在秋天再見個面，以便討論細節。

如我所答應的，這是羅傑的電子郵件地址：
rogerchen88@yoyodyne.com.tw.。他知道您會寫信給他，他會非常樂意幫忙。
如果有任何疑問，請告訴我。

克莉斯汀

Part
11
後續

143 電子郵件的樣本 IV
Sample Email IV

From : Edward
To : Cynthia

Cynthia,

I just wanted to thank you again for coming. I hope you and your group had a comfortable stay.

Bad news! One of your bags got left behind at our office. Please send me an address and we'll mail it to you right away. As soon as you're back and settled in,[1] let's schedule a time to chat.

Until then,
Edward

143 電子郵件的樣本 IV
Sample Email IV

寄件人：艾德華
收件人：辛希雅

辛希雅：

我只是要再次謝謝您的來訪。我希望您和您的團隊在參訪期間都過得愉快。

有個不好的消息！您掉了一個包包在我們辦公室。請寄個地址給我，我們會立刻將包包寄回給您。等您一到家並且安頓好，我們就安排一個時間聊聊。

到時候見了。

艾德華

Word
List

1 settle in 安頓下來；習慣於

國家圖書館出版品預行編目資料

迎賓 900 句典 / Brian Greene 作：
——初版.——臺北市：貝塔，2007〔民 96〕
    面；   公分

  ISBN 978-957-729-645-0（平裝附光碟片）

  1. 英國英語—會話

805.188   96004328

迎賓 900 句典

Overheard While Entertaining Guests

作   者 / Brian Greene
總 編 審 / 王復國
譯   者 / 林曉芳
執行編輯 / 官芝羽、杜文田

出   版 / 貝塔出版有限公司
地   址 / 台北市 100 館前路 12 號 11 樓
電   話 / (02)2314-2525
傳   真 / (02)2312-3535
郵   撥 / 19493777 貝塔出版有限公司
客服專線 / (02)2314-3535
客服信箱 / btservice@betamedia.com.tw

總 經 銷 / 時報文化出版企業股份有限公司
地   址 / 桃園縣龜山鄉萬壽路二段 351 號
電   話 / (02) 2306-6842

出版日期 / 2007 年 4 月初版一刷
定   價 / 250 元
I S B N：978-957-729-645-0

Overheard While Entertaining Guests by Brian Greene
Copyright 2007 by Beta Multimedia Publishing
Published by Beta Multimedia Pubishing

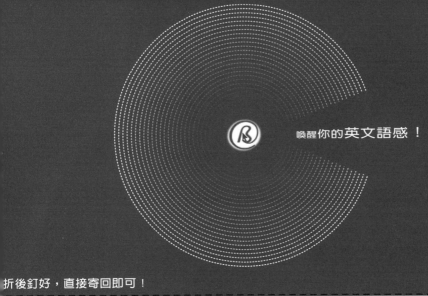

喚醒你的英文語感！

折後釘好，直接寄回即可！

100 台北市中正區館前路12號11樓

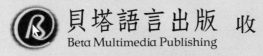 貝塔語言出版 收
Beta Multimedia Publishing

寄件者住址 □ □ □

讀者服務專線（02）2314-3535　讀者服務傳真（02）2312-3535
客戶服務信箱　btservice@betamedia.com.tw

www.betamedia.com.tw

謝謝您購買本書！！

貝塔語言擁有最優良之英文學習書籍，為提供您最佳的英語學習資訊，您填妥此表後寄回（免貼郵票）將可不定期免費收到本公司最新發行書訊及活動訊息！

姓名：＿＿＿＿＿＿＿＿＿＿　性別：□男 □女　生日：＿＿＿＿年＿＿＿＿月＿＿＿＿日

電話：(公)＿＿＿＿＿＿＿＿(宅)＿＿＿＿＿＿＿＿(手機)＿＿＿＿＿＿＿＿

電子信箱：＿＿＿＿＿＿＿＿＿＿＿＿＿＿＿＿＿＿

學歷：□高中職含以下 □專科 □大學 □研究所含以上

職業：□金融 □服務 □傳播 □製造 □資訊 □軍公教 □出版 □自由 □教育 □學生 □其他

職級：□企業負責人 □高階主管 □中階主管 □職員 □專業人士

1. 您購買的書籍是？＿＿＿＿＿＿＿＿＿＿＿＿＿＿＿＿＿＿

2. 您從何處得知本產品？(可複選)

　　　□書店 □網路 □書展 □校園活動 □廣告信函 □他人推薦 □新聞報導 □其他

3. 您覺得本產品價格：

　　　□偏高 □合理 □偏低

4. 請問目前您每週花了多少時間學英語？

　　　□不到十分鐘 □十分鐘以上，但不到半小時 □半小時以上，但不到一小時

　　　□一小時以上，但不到兩小時 □兩個小時以上 □ 不一定

5. 通常在選擇語言學習書時，哪些因素是您會考慮的？

　　　□ 封面 □內容、實用性 □品牌 □媒體、朋友推薦 □價格 □其他＿＿＿＿＿＿＿

6. 市面上您最需要的語言書種類為？

　　　□聽力 □閱讀 □文法 □口說 □寫作 □其他＿＿＿＿＿＿＿

7. 通常您會透過何種方式選購語言學習書籍？

　　　□書店門市 □網路書店 □郵購 □直接找出版社 □學校或公司團購

　　　□其他＿＿＿＿＿＿＿

8. 給我們的建議：＿＿＿＿＿＿＿＿＿＿＿＿＿＿＿＿＿＿＿＿＿＿＿＿

＿＿＿＿＿＿＿＿＿＿＿＿＿＿＿＿＿＿＿＿＿＿＿＿＿＿＿＿＿＿＿＿

喚醒你的英文語感！

Get a Feel for English !